This novel was created by computer software called ALMA for Artificial Linguistic Machine Algorithm programmed by David Cope over many years and described in detail in his book *Computer Generated Novels* (2020). ALMA is capable of producing over two-and-a-half quintillion other novels without human intervention except selecting the database and initiating the software to do so usually taking less than a few seconds per book.

Darkest Hour

By

ALMA

A Computer Generated Novel

David Cope

Darkest Hour

A Novel

By ALMA

David Cope

Epoc Books

Printed in the United States of America

Published 2020.

The characters and events in this book are fictitious.
Any similarity to real persons, living or dead, is coincidental
and not intended by the authors.

CHAPTER 1.

While driving, Francis got a handle on it; he hadn't seen a fundamental piece of the land. Not really. Here, little pines and strange terrain came close to the persistently moving inclinations. Green even in winter.

The cloudless sky made his capabilities further sharpened.

A marvelous scene.

He drove a few more miles and stopped close to the road with the motor, despite everything, cooling and unpredictably ticking simultaneously. He left the vehicle, shut its door, and strolled a quarter mile or something along those lines. At long last, to the extent conceivable, he walked through open spaces without ponds of dissolved snow interceding. Chaparral zone with pinion reaching the fields.

Nothing exceptional about this specific zone. He could have journeyed one-additional mile and likely discovered the same; it wouldn't have had any different kind of effect. Nevertheless, the quiet and nonappearance of hindrances with an unpredictable breeze, and the sun slipping and trailing a cloud made it grandly amazing. In any event for him.

Finding a grassless spot, he sat with his legs crossed and him content. Something he hadn't created in many years.

Looking at anything at all appeared to supportively end up being all-satisfactory here. Being a bit of the land and sky, not a visitor to it.

He glanced upward and saw a bird overhead scanning for lunch, he recognized, and getting a charge out of going any place the breeze took it, rather than attempting to induce the breeze to take it to a particular spot.

He was unable to discover comfort, in imagining what it might take after up there. Free as a feathered animal. Regardless of the way that he understood it wasn't generous. Expected to eat, breed, and fight with contenders.

For him, unpredictable and anguishing duties took him reliably.

During the second swipe, it showed they were one. Two spirits breathing everything; a tantamount air and unpretentiously superb, dreaming on an amazing snowless winter day in North Dakota.

He looked down and found a solitary piece of turf looking out of the earth alongside him, in any event a foot if not two against some other soil spread. A loner, like him.

Looking up again, he saw the bird of prey again. Separated from the rest. This one getting a charge out of an uncommon look at light before freezing in the following winter storm.

A slight breeze brushed his cheek like several supple lips might. Not a kiss, yet a teasingly botched chance. He looked upward once again.

The winged creature had evaporated.

That's when he heard it. The sort of sound offering no hint of the distance away it had begun. A moderate blast close by, or a staggeringly solid eruption in a far range.

No smoke or signs of its source.

Then it vanished.

Having his succinct dream so impolitely meddled with, he stood and progressed bit by bit back to his car.

As he contemplated it, he bent over to be emphatically aware of the differentiation among disengagement and control. The sound had started from the upper east. An impact. Most likely daily practice around here. Oil nation. Infiltrating. Fracking. Who figured that out?

At the point when he arrived at the vehicle, he found a flying animal's equivalent to the fowl he'd seen had left a calling card on the hood. A white spot, uncovering to him what he thought of his interference. Or then again, so it showed up. Most likely a basic organic need, not a statement of supposition. In any case, it rose as if it were the perfect hour to get himself back to the human advancement he was used to, and appearance whatever the madding jams there had figured to him.

As he drove away, he gazed again at the pines and prairie. To what extent had it been like this? What's more, to what degree would it take mankind to suit it into an option that is other than what's normal and less one of a kind.

The car he drove, not his, made successful time and he was back home before he knew it. He would have pulled out his laptop-computer and looked through the web had he anything to examine for.

Joe was the main name they'd given the man. He was the lawful advocate. How many legal counselors in the nation had been named Joe? He didn't need to recognize it. Fifty million dollars appeared to be extremely incredible, diverged from the concession he'd gotten for his examination over the previous decade.

Be that as it may, at what cost would this help come? Precisely he'd lose his dependability. Most likely lose his psychological adequacy worrying over spending an unbelievable leftover portion in prison. Who perceived what else?

He wouldn't do it. Couldn't do it.

He proceeded to bed to forget about it, he requested himself.

In any event, the underlying portion.

What to do? Go to Patton and mention to him what had occurred?

Whether or not if he could discover these people, they'd deny it. Regardless of whether he communicated with them about the expense to computer clients, what might that achieve? They hadn't really completed any idea yet about devising an arrangement. Was there a law against that?

He didn't know their names, simply inconclusive portrayals.

Patton had community police power and bunches of understudies doing idiotic duties these days. Taking lots of cop-hours.

Possibly, he could go to the parochial columnists. Make a tolerable story. Perchance could get by the wire administrations. At the point when it was out there, what would his guests do?

He had no notion of their character. That wouldn't make the paper editors happy. The sum total of what he had was an ideal little plot achieved by a social occasion of three men to make billions of dollars against spreading a PC virus that would not unquestionably hurt any computer, simply make its customer unglued as a hornet for a period. After that they'd fix it so it wouldn't happen again for ten bucks a pop. Like an establishment stunt.

But it could make them a fortune, many occasions over.

Endlessly he went attempting one potential arrangement and next expansion. Each time he accepted, he had concern, but no luck.

His guests had set this up, and reasonably he'd give them that. Was he the man they required?

Likely.

Would it work?

Likely.

Did he need the money for his investigation?

Indeed.

Did it hurt anyone?

Yes. To a degree in any event. Not unending truly.

And neighboring he went.

No, apparently. No other likely decision than when he'd begun.

At three in the afternoon, he decided to change his insights to Cassie Davies, their school town's head librarian and his own real sentiment. Other than Patton and Jackson, an accomplice of his in the mind study of his home office. She was the principle singular he trusted completely. An ideal cure to his present quandary welcomed by his trio of guests.

Until a minute ago, he would call her directly, yet thinking about her was unwinding. Or, on the other hand, it energized him in a manner not quite the same as that which had additionally kept him wakeful.

He finally took a few sleeping pills. He'd put something aside for such an occasion, and fell napping to dream of Cassie. A fantasy damnation; mind his own business thank you in full.

His underlying acceptance when he woke and looked at the clock revealing to him it was ten-thirty in the morning which was that he'd be held for his seven stars of daylight. That is, in the event that he had one.

It was a Saturday. So, he lay in his bed and attempted to remember Friday and it returned to him.

The furious person named Patton. What's more, the three folks with the recommendation. Ten minutes. Generally. That was all it had taken.

He took his hour in the shower, cut his facial hair, and made supper or whatever he liked to call it. Espresso introductory, and not long after eggs and toast.

He took as an unending hour, as essential to eating to start the three days end of the week night. The kitchen opening gave him a scowl at a shady sky, yet no snowflakes falling he could see. Cold decisively, however sheltered.

He didn't wish to own an automobile, so he walked everywhere throughout the area. That could be unsafe, given the regular, yet having a vehicle didn't make things significantly more straightforward. He could consistently walk where others couldn't drive.

He took transports to go longer separations. Significantly more secure than attempting to surf on the oftentimes cold and brave streets.

Finally, he called Cassie on the landline to hear her point of view of what his Friday could mean. She consistently had bits of information that avoided him. She didn't answer much after twelve rings. Presumably out for a walk or visiting a companion.

While an extraordinary few people would inspect their climate, an issue North Dakotans noticed splendidly like weather. Indeed, even commendable. Ideal for taking the pooch out to incorporate a few aromas or shopping.

They had shaped a few several feet beginning close to the edge of the timberland where Cassie and he had caused their underlying plot to hightail it to opportunity. Or, on the other hand, so they by then had an idea this might work.

Francis saw her back the farthest away and investigated the crowd attempting to find him.

Still not feeling his new look would deceive him, he evaded his head and Cassie's likewise and they stopped. He and Cassie inconspicuously next dissipated into the woodlands. No one developed the scarcest piece interested by their escape, so lost in their own one of a kind, worries over what direction the gang may chase them.

Checking what thirty-six stories vertical drop may mean when laid on the dirt and imagining some bit of the radio tower hammering their ears, he helped Cassie down to the brook that had been dry the last he'd ventured along these lines. It had loaded up with spring precipitation, yet at the same time represented no issue.

Water perchance an inch deep.

They crossed it and progressed up to street level to join the rest of genuine sovereigns. Not all that terrible as of recently.

But where to go? He couldn't follow a similar course as he had so far. They'd absolutely search for them there first. He asked her what direction. She took a look at him curiously and pointed to one side. He went right. She went left. She didn't really care at that point.

They both strolled snappy yet didn't run. No reason to cause others to notice themselves. Traffic was light anyway, with everyone having cellphones, and any anything peculiar may cause a 911 call.

He battled to remain underneath the streetlights. Like each component so far, it, despite everything, appeared to be ideal to do the specific inverse of what came as common.

Let everyone watch them moving for a late-night walk together. Altogether better than anybody worry getting a glance at two people walking in the forest along the walkway but in different directions.

In the long run, they arrived at a go-across road and left the woods. They each entered one zone of little stores generally of the articles of clothing in character. Everybody had shut off their lights in the lofts above them.

So far, he noted that he had no conspicuous evidence that Cassie was now in visual sight. They needed to escape the light before an inactive cop cruiser passed by and pulled them in.

Once they were both found, the cops would easily recognize Francis since his mug was on the front pages of every city newspaper and he'd be arrested and placed in prison as New York City's biggest murderer in their history.

He charged into the essential rear entryway that showed up. What's more, into their essential merchant of the night-time. "What's your pleasure, pal?"

His eyes hadn't acclimated to the night yet. But that wasn't his biggest problem, nor was the potential arrest. His most pressing difficulty was 'where was Cassie?' How had he lost her? Could he find her? Was she alright?

In Queens in the dead of night, without Cassie along and safe.

He could hardly make out the image of a man standing in front of him holding an attaché case with no vulnerability and bested with an approach to selling dope that destroyed lives.

"Hello mate. I know you." And Francis fathomed that by some chance they'd caught a similar seller of weeks past. He'd anywise remembered him even without his whiskers. "Where's your woman companion? I remember you like those meth tubes. Am I right?"

"What?"

"I got some of the best in here."

Francis then educated him to get lost, and to come to the meaningful conclusion giving him the effective purpose of his hand against his sanctuary. Insufficient to truly hurt him, but rather only enough to make him rest the remainder of the darkest hour.

He turned and went the only way he could go, back the way they had come.

He headed down the rear entryway against the sparkle and the oblivious vendor. He gazed cautiously to one side, ideal for different spots that could get him some place not on display of sneaking squad cars.

Obviously, sovereigns shouldn't deal with the expense of such places.

His lone decision was to turn at the following road. He predicted he'd find a good section of town. Or, on the other hand, a restaurant zone. Both of those would have near back streets, if for no other reason than to dispose of their trash.

He saw a clog of townhouses around two streets away. Lamentably, a few men all wearing group tones loose against a lamppost truly in their manner. Mind blowing.

He turned toward the left and away from them. Three of the pack looked clearly at him. At any rate, no cops in the locale. In the event that these were truly storm people as he suspected, they'd have vulnerability or posts with cellphones checking the local police close by.

By and by, all through twenty feet among them in any case, no guns he could see. Or him against tire irons, blackjacks, or chains.

Blades.

Most likely.

"Yo home. Meeting you here."

I looked him in his eyes.

"Communicate in English, blockhead."

He looked at Francis like a natural.

Francis truly confronted them. All of them. Assault. No other method to battle. Amazing.

He'd make a model of the leader.

The gang-leader pulled out a sharp edge and brought it up so Francis could watch it. Yet, his eyes parted with him. The leader was inconclusive and unsure about his walk. His glare went to words.

One possibility. Get lost or you're toast. He looked next to him and saw his hypothetical siblings holding on to cut him up.

A state of respect.

The incorrect concern.

By then he'd contacted him and planted one foot into his correct knee as he brought his left elbow up legitimately into his chest and his elbow upward to his jaw.

He battled to holler, yet the fast implosion of his lungs made it sound like a frog croaking. No chance to point his cutting edge concerning him, so he palmed it, beginning him as he dropped to the black-top. Unreasonably straightforward.

Now he gazed at the pack.

One less.

Likewise again, he wandered authentically confronting them at an even pace. Nothing in his air aside from certainty.

They overviewed with building anxiety as he moved closer. He exhibited no fear at that point. Only interest about what plan he had for their executions.

Damnation, even he would have run.

Potentially they were inept. Or on the other hand, too bewildered over what had just happened. So quickly.

Next, they ran.

In a different heading, no less. No cooperation. The posse attitude quickly lost in the midst of everything.

He stopped at the corner and looked back at Cassie who wasn't there.

He felt very confident about himself, to such a degree as he'd been successful so far.

Except for where Cassie was at this moment, and that was more of challenge than the gang leader's simple and childish challenge.

CHAPTER 2.

Francis spent two days searching for Cassie in Queens but without luck. He was hungry, tired, despondent, and afraid for Cassie as he found his way back to the Christopher Masters' Building. Cassie had been kidnapped, captured by Masters he guessed, still lost, or being forced by the police to help them find Francis, a serial killer according to all but those who had taken her against her will.

Strolling toward the lift entryways, he saw the watchman already busy phoning the floor where CM could be found. At that point, down the metal bar stepping stool and he'd be in the mystery zone. Might it be that simple? Was that where they were keeping her?

He endeavored to pull the entryways apart.

No go.

In any event, not in the way he'd worked it previously. By then he remembered Cassandra and his past obstructed escape. How had he situated himself? To the other side hand, sticking to the ladder, and climbing with one hand. He endeavored to reflect it and presto it worked. The entryways gradually stripped back uncovering the vacant deep opening. The up-rising above, in spite of everything, he'd climbed and anyway catapulted the blasting chamber making it easier to hear.

The stepping stool focal was the place it had been that day.

Anxious to recognize that something hadn't changed, he grabbed the rail and maneuvered himself focal the pole and onto the rungs.

Straightforward.

Presently he needed to trust the lift wouldn't exude down and hang over the entryway he'd just radiated through. No entryways in the base of the vehicle, just at the top. No real way to find a workable pace, it was above him when he battled. This time he'd be stuck down in the basement until somebody chose to take it once more. Could be some time given that the greater part of the crowd on the thirteenth floor waited extra regularly than not.

He chose to hazard it, and down he climbed. Exactly when his foot hit base, he bent and saw the best approach to enter the lift that had been emptied and the path was absolutely liberated from square one. Dim, so he couldn't see what shocks it possibly could uncover.

Be that as it may, he was directly down regardless.

Did some other individual acknowledge how basic this was? Did they visit here frequently? Or on the other hand, ever?

He circumspectly crept closer to the entryway and promptly got a smelly scent that helped him to remember his grandmother's house when he was a child.

Mothballs.

Smelled consummately like those.

Toxic substance utilized for warding moths off cloth. Perchance this was the place all the old garbs were kept.

As his eyes acclimated to the darkness, he made out what resembled a gleaming light at a boundlessness. Like a radiator pilot light.

The insignificant certainty that he could see that far made him presume the spot was vacant. However, never state Francis didn't have inventive vitality, for in any case he accepted how possible it was that huge limit holders lay to the other side and right, gathering the circulation community in the Indiana Jones's films, where the *Lost Ark* was set away amidst a few other conceivably huge memorabilia kept by the governing body.

He wandered into the room, the aroma finding a good pace grounded as he did. Still wouldn't notice anything.

So, he connected two hands, the extent that his arms would take them.

Nothing. Just air and that smell. The last so solid since he hacked multiple times. What else would someone use mothballs for other than pesticide? Long haul introduction can make all approaches to hurt living things. Counting people. Doable, they utilized these for dealing with rodents and other vermin just as moths.

By then he reviewed his science. Naphthalene and paradichlorobenzene were the primary elements of mothballs.

On the off chance that memory served, they could be mixed in with various manufactured products that can be used in explicit gases to make WMDS. Weapons of mass destruction. Was that what this was about?

The stench began to make him feel wiped out.

No longer down here he let himself know.

He strolled across the room and arrived at the pilot light.

Adequately sure it was a bit of a radiator or something to that effect. By then, before he got a chance to come to an undeniable end result, the damn thing contacted startling the shit out of him. An immense thunder and the smell of mothballs evaporated with the new smell of combustible gas.

Besides, the room completely lit up. He modified, hoping to recognize some extraordinary disclosure. What's more, he did. Nothing. The room was totally vacant. His little demonstration gone to hellfire and beyond.

He looked about for some sort of tell that anything else was out of order. Or, on the other hand, a hint of whatever would recommend what its past substance may have been. Very little.

Concrete dividers. No sheets. No canvases of disfigured bodies on the dividers, or blood trickling from the roof. For this situation, catch a passage up to the principal floor.

A specific something should stand out enough to be noticed. A tremendous section by the huge heater. Roundabout and maybe three feet wide, moving bit by bit upward at around a twenty-degree edge. Wires and trunk lines leaving it before entering a breaker box on the divider.

An exit plan.

Unquestionably, adequate, enormous enough for a man to crawl inside. What's more, it would need to rise to at some point significant.

An electric plant? Not likely. That could be miles out there.

Conceivably one-progressively greater entry. No intimation, however it offered the best course for escape he'd experienced up until now.

With that bit of data achieved, he worked his way back over the room, snappier this time taking into account the light permitted it, and the lift chute returned.

Thank God, the lift vehicle had stayed on the thirteenth or something floor high above, and he ascended the stepping stool again, pulled the primary floor entryways separated, and inside two or three minutes pressed the catch to ride back up to the lab and his room.

Cassandra was sitting at her workstation as usual when he showed up. Made no undertaking to accept a look at him as he entered the lab. He crossed to his station, plunked down, and took a shot at the first form of the infection.

The inquiry was the manner in which would he harm this variant so they couldn't run over what he'd done. Possibly include a clock. Try not to show this sheet going before such and such a period. Something to that effect.

As he worked, his musings bent to his Cassie. What was going on in North Dakota these days? To what extent had he been no more.

In any event, it had now been seven days. Presumably not exactly a quarter of a month. Adequately long that without telling anyone his cautious whereabouts, someone should have gotten focused. Besides higher, what was proceeding onward in fact out there? Legislative issue wars, most bursting films, and so on?

Cooped up didn't spread what he felt directly by then.

No accepted way how his Cassie felt about him, yet she must be somewhere he could find her. Considering their commitment, she'd been hard to comprehend. Likely educating the supervisor about everything he might do. Some portion of the group alongside the remainder of them. He pondered breaking for opportunity. When to do it? Directions to prepare.

His greatest stress was keeping warm. He had no jacket or other method to fight off the winter temperatures when he rose up out of the passage. Needed to deal with that before he made his run again.

At that point, he mulled over his money-related issues. He'd burned through the entirety of his enormous bills on Cassandra's propensity. Plausibly, he still had two or three dollars left for a gala or two, and even more essentially a few pennies here and there.

Then again, where was his wallet? Not on him for sure. Without a doubt, he'd demonstrated a few times he didn't recall seeing it in his room. No coins in his pockets and no distinctive confirmation.

He found a workable space station and progressed back to the room and chased it down. No luck. Without an approach to keep warm, no cash, and no distinguishing proof of identity, how far would he get? The loss of even one of those could put him in prison no less right back here. He needed to find his wallet. At the point when he last had it. When he'd hauled it out of his pocket to pay the pusher. Before he rested to the sound of Cassandra's determined babbling that night. After that no further wallet.

No one had come to visit the lab since he'd been back. Strange.

Where was CM at a time like this? Why not in this room with him asking for a demonstration, asking him where he'd been for three days, and how had he escaped the building with his lovely Cassie in hand?

CHAPTER 3.

Francis's mind jumped back to a time in which a young lady screamed for help in the snow-driven meadow outside the Computer Science Building because she'd been shot in the back and the only person in a position to help was Francis himself. She died, supposedly, and her death became a complete confusion with two other young ladies looking like her also getting involved.

Lucky for Francis, everything turned out alright with Cassie, the one shot, turned out to be part of a plot to reveal a group of terrorists. And with that memory, he sat and did his best not to cry. Could she be a casualty a second time?

Francis plodded through a snow bank next to the sidewalk to circumvent slipping on a slim layer of slippery ice that had formed there. Twenty yards or so from the front strides to his original destination, he heard her screaming for help. She'd run out of gas and gave Francis the idea she couldn't go any further.

Help rushed the young lady's failing call.

He couldn't overlook her pleas. Francis could hardly hear her voice any longer. She seemed to drop onto the snow and wither.

He caught her just before she struck the ground. After picking her up and looking into her face, she seemed to plead with him with her eyes. Simultaneously, Francis saw his hands behind her had turned glue-like and her eyes collapsed up into her head like somebody losing consciousness.

He shouted, "What's happening?"

The snow around her had turned bright red.

Her blood poured out of her relentlessly. Something was wrong. Truly off-base.

He grabbed her under her knees and holding his forearm to support her head, picked her up and walked as quickly as he could back toward the C-S building.

Who was she?

Her blood flowed dark red and turning black as he watched. The essence of life seeped from her body onto the top shelf of the ice and buried itself beneath her. God be with her.

'Don't die,' he told her, not that it did anything helpful. Speed was of key importance. Though still breathing, she didn't move. Francis focused on keeping her alive.

As he ran her toward the building, Francis looked behind him and saw that the man he'd seen before was gone, yet his footprints were still noticeable.

He looked around for someone to aid him and her. A few understudies strolled toward the structure where he'd strode minutes previous.

He waved his arms to make them observe.

"She's fading."

His point made two males hurry in his direction. Pointing at one, Francis ordered him to call 911. The other he told to help him carry the girl. The two of them complied. After all, he was faculty and they students. Academic pecking order and all that.

We got her up the steps to the C-S building, through the double doors and into the warm faux-marble foyer.

As the door closed behind them, he could hear their footsteps resonate in the mausoleum-like room.

Francis and the student laid her down cautiously in a pool of blood that had just started leaking underneath her. The understudy who'd helped him convey her inside summed up the circumstance, "Crap, she's hurt terribly. What happened?"

He did as well as he possibly could. No thought. She'd called for help. The tension was bound tightly. No sign of any life left. Blacking out and vanishing quickly.

He yelled for help.

Nobody moved even a miniscule.

Was he dead? Had to be. The gas causing an unnatural weather difference made his infection assault carbon-dioxide, one of the four noteworthy ozone depleting substances—others being nitrous oxide, water vapor, and methane—the human form of any living form couldn't exist without.

Does that make sense?

He struggled to open his eyes. Couldn't. As full as he willed them to do as such they wouldn't. Actually made everything worse trying, so he stopped.

'God,' he commented. Turned out extra than the right balance of CO_2, and they sickened from global warming and less than the right balance of CO_2, and then they just died. A sensitive yet basic climatic harmony.

Obviously, it didn't make him feel any better knowing the infection that had him was his own creation. His fingernails hurt. Every one of his hair follicles hurt. His teeth ached. Indeed, even his watch hurt.

Nonetheless, he was certain that wasn't part of him and he wouldn't actually feel it regardless of to what extent he'd worn it.

He then experienced someone touch him.

It hurt.

Damn, why contact him. Let him be. He wanted to die. Deserved to die. Whatever.

He imagined what kind of drugs would make this pain stop. Co2? Why hadn't somebody given him his torment executioners.

He deserved to die, yes, but not like this.

He dreamt for genuine this time. If one can dream for real.

Wherever he was, it was damn cold.

The mists encompassing him spun as a tornado might against the bursting power of the night.

In the focal point of the vortex above him, he could pinpoint an eye. A solitary and gigantic unblinking eye.

Staring at him in the most unforgiving way possible.

At that point, a most unrealistic thing happened. An enormous tear framed in a side of that eye and it cried on Francis. It doused him in its distress, and he couldn't breathe. He was suffocating.

What's added, he woke. The hail tornado and the eye were gone. In their spot was a cool dim room colder than any room in a lodging as decent as this one ought to be.

Everything was incorrect.

Out of point.

He wondered whether or not the dead Bill had informed his mercenary troops that the 'kill Francis' order had been rescinded. Or were they now forming outside the hotel, each coveting the reward he'd undoubtedly placed on Francis's head.

Did he hazard making a sound?

Were Cassie and Patton in the next room gambling cards?

Why was it so damn cold? As was constant, a lot of greater number of inquiries than answers.

He decided to sit up. Gave him a better perspective.

So, he did.

Seeing now the whole room in obscurity, he could make out different corners and edges of tables, and seats and casements.

Still murky though.

He changed position and glanced out through the venetian blinds behind him. The delicate sparkle of streetlights, yet nothing else. No other lights anywhere. It was as if the town had died. Or gotten sick.

His infection had struck Canada, no doubt. And found its way here.

He went back into the room. Woozy though acceptable. By now his eyes had adjusted to the night and he could see more clearly. Nothing routine registered.

Next, he saw it. Or its absence. He walked over and stared at the rug, his eyes forthcoming, accustomed to the darkness.

No indication of it. No nothing anything. They couldn't have cleaned Bill's blood so thoroughly and that quickly.

He reached down and experienced the carpet. Smooth as silk. As if nothing had taken place here at all. The room looked fine regardless of how hard he endeavored to criticize it. Had he, by one way or addition, envisioned the whole thing? Originating where? When had he strolled to the drugstore to make the phone call? Sometime before Bill's pistol had poked him in the spine? Had he envisioned he'd in some way or one-more enrolled and gone to a room and nodded off? Was that even conceivable? And was the world dead? And he the only one still living in it? If so, why was he still here?

Further inquiries. Would he be able to have built up an insusceptibility some way or another? Be that as it may, he was a professional.

He meandered around the room searching for signs Bill had been there. Where was someone called

Christopher Masters who'd likely shot and killed him. Cassie and Patton had originated from North Dakota to save him. But the room wouldn't comfort him to invoke such a picture.

Crawling back to the sofa, he plunked himself down. 'Death come to me now,' he thought. He didn't want to die, but he prayed for it to happen. No matter how it would arrive, don't spare him.

And then he experienced something strange. A delicate quality on his lips. A recollection. It was a moist and enticing kiss. The kiss of forgiveness. Originating from God. He laid back and fell napping again.

But the lips reached down to the soles of his feet and back again.

Insistent and yet gentle.

The second daylight back in his apartment in North Dakota after most every element had quieted, he comprehended what an idiot he'd been. He needn't have worried about his virus turning on humans after all. Each had been constructed dependent on Asimov's Three Laws. Crave independence. Respect all lifeforms. Develop.

The second law, like the second law of thermodynamics, was a corker. The infection shouldn't assault others regardless of the transformations that may originate to pass for it. As though this were not disclosure enough, Cassie visited and told him they were to be hitched in a couple of months.

The date hadn't passed as he believed it had. He was looking forward to it, he told her. And he implied it. After all, the constant tug on his testosterone taking meeting beautiful women would end and he could concentrate only on her and his research.

In any event, he imagined that would be the situation, driving him to contemplate Cassandra. After all, he wasn't married yet. Of the steady number of individuals he'd met and worked with amid the years he'd spent inquiring about counterfeit and genuine life, she was the most confounding. He realized he'd endeavored to manage her.

In any case, perchance he should be able to. But who the hell was she? Would he ever observe her again? On his side or on another side or on no side by any means? He'd have to talk to his psychologist about her.

Jackson or Cassie?

CHAPTER 4.

Where was Cassie now? And with whom? Both the good and bad guys were after Francis. Was she still in Queens, hiding out? Or back in North Dakota, safe and sound? But either way, why hadn't she called him? Was she still being interviewed by the cops? About him mostly? Or in prison as a co-conspirator in the murders? Was she dead? And with that thought, Francis broke down sobbing.

The next morning, he woke not hearing ten lords a-leaping. But they no uncertainty were there. Somewhere at any rate.

He was up early, though not early enough to beat Patton.

As they ate breakfast, Francis informed him that he couldn't put anyone at risk for harboring a fugitive any longer, and forced him to take a few bucks to help pay for what he'd eaten.

He disclosed to him what an incredible person he'd been to have confidence in him, gathered his sack, and was out the entryway before early afternoon seeing the sky had blurred over.

One-more storm on its way, no uncertainty precisely when it looked like a great atmospheric phenomenon had originated to remain for some time.

He had no suspicion about what to do, where to go, or whom to believe in at this moment. Perchance he could catch a bus out of town.

No. They'd have that secured just as the trains. No airports for a hundred miles in any direction. Three hotels in town, but they'd have those looked after, too.

That's when it ensued to him that the former late area they'd think he'd go was right back where he began. Home. His condo down the street. Near by. At least he could go there and see if they had the area guarded. If not, and he kept the lights at dark, and didn't leave during the day, it could work. Worth an attempt.

He took the back way. It felt great to charge ahead again and not fleeing. His physique absolutely sensed-it like itself. No all the higher limping. No other reaction except sorry for himself. Hour to step up to the retained.

When he came around the back of his area, he saw him quickly. Patton still had his place secured with a cop out back. Probably one out front as well. Such a large count of policemen squandering their time searching for a guiltless observer who'd done concerning himself incorrectly.

He was directly starting over originating the originating.

Later it occurred to him that possibly he had it mistaken. If he could hold up until after dark, he may locate an internal hallway and advance past the gatekeepers and innermost. Once there, they'd never think to search for him in his very own place. After all, how could he get in there without them seeing him? And why would he want to go there in the first place?

So, he found a decent area to hide unseen, spent the rest of the daytime wishing he'd stayed until dusk to avoid all the wasted time.

Hours passed slowly.

But the sun ran-away and the cop, the only one he could observe, was relieved of duty by one-more cop, one on the younger side.

Rather than move to avoid the foretold snow and breeze, he tended apropos huddling in one point looking around once in a while though without abundant conviction. Over eight, he found the right corridor, made his way down it as if it were everything extra than a routine return against an early dinner, avoided the cop, and entered his apartment with his key like nothing unusual at all.

He shut the entryway subsequently behind him as quietly as he could, locked it, breathed a yawning sigh of relief, and, knowing he shouldn't turn on the lights, worked his way toward the pantry.

He recognized now how to arrive. The great-sized aluminum barn it seemed looked empty.

He backtracked next to an enormous oak stand and laid himself down behind it. He could still observe the warehouse and most of the open meadow around it, but was also lying on ice. Even with his numerous coats on, he could feel the bitter cold against his chest.

They retained to the probe whether anything changed in the event that somebody gave him away and they adhered up progressively.

Ten minutes passed.

Everything changed that he could see. Apparently the same for Jackson as he'd made no movements apropos him, no extraordinary sign whatever that may be.

The structure truly appeared vacant. Obviously taken this separation, it could have been loaded with wild elephants without him knowing the distinction. All he needed was some style of proof the spot was involved; a shadow, a light rushing on, or a sound, even a delicate one. But zilch suggested the spot was occupied, or that anyone stood guard to shelter the perimeter.

He and Jackson waited a long half hour and still no sign. An exercise in futility to him, yet who knew?

Next, out of nowhere, an agitation. He was certain about it.

'Jackson,' he whispered. He was also waving for him to move in somewhat closer. They crawled toward the spot, yet at the same time spread out wanting to terrify them to extermination.

Not likely, but maybe.

Ten additional yards of woods secured, and a superior perspective on the structure and encompassing accessible territory. Still no explicit sign of occupation.

They waited longer. As they did, he saw something odd. Voices, or if nobody else, he believed to such an extent. He heard a radio out there, nonetheless without music. Couldn't make sure what he was hearing, though absolutely normal to the backwoods in which they lay. No birds or frogs or anything else flora delivered in this cold lonely and forsaken point.

Jackson offered him the go-ahead indication. He returned it. Something was happening.

A solitary gatekeeper getting paid the lowest pay permitted by law tuning in to a radio syndicated program or fear-based oppressors making arrangements to annihilate the world. Or any of the possibilities that lay between those two extremes.

Progress.

He gave his shoulders an up-down activity; the universal what-the-fuck sign for Jackson to see.

Jackson smiled, and reappeared to look and listen. He'd heard the same.

Then he realized they'd hit pay dirt. A shadow cut the lower corner of one of the windows and quickly vanished. He was certain of it. He stared over at Jackson. He'd clearly seen it, too. A guard extending his legs or one of the fear mongers showing signs of improvement on the edge of their situation.

To pick them off one by one with his long-run rifle.

Jackson mouthed everything to him, exaggerating his silent pronunciation of each word to make himself understood.

Obstacle was, regardless of his absurd intrigues, he didn't have the slightest idea what he was endeavoring to state.

Again, he gave the universal what-the-fuck sign.

He shook his head and waved once apropos the distribution center. The universal go-get-yourself-killed sign.

They drew nearer.

Could Cassie be inside with these idiots? Was she still alive?

He still couldn't have seen anyone outside guarding the warehouse. The casements were opaque, at least to them, so no way to identify individuals except for shadows on the glass. The voices had gotten louder, though he still couldn't make out any words. Likely not a radio syndicated program; no ads, and intermittent long quiet spots.

At least two people were innermost making the watchman a less likely possibility. If the place was empty, who needed two to guard it? In truth, who required one to monitor it?

He indicated to Jackson for guidance. What to do straightaway?

Jackson had zero to suggest. In actuality, he noticed like he'd overlooked he was there. How to get his attention if he weren't looking? They hadn't covered that.

Getting up on one knee stood out enough to be noticed. He pushed his palms descending, demonstrating he should lie down.

After a fashion, the spot didn't appear to be especially compromising, so he remained the manner in which he was not that he would have stood up and waved his hands. He just couldn't imagine anyone noticing him on one knee. Besides, the voices proceeded continuously. Assuredly, if he'd been spotted there, it would have created a delay, or an animating, or anything to show a break in routine, yet the patter proceeded as though nobody had taken note.

They waited.

No added shadows, so they waited some more.

Closing in on four in the afternoon, three hours before his scheduled meeting with the grad students.

He decided to take a chance.

Without signaling Jackson, he turned and crawled his way back to a point where the road narrowed. Once there, he lay flat on his stomach and pulled his way slowly throughout the cold mud inch-by-inch and centimeter-by-centimeter. It took about five minutes to make the journey.

He figured nobody could have seen him do it, not in any case Jackson.

Once crosswise over, he slithered toward his place. Easier target or not, he needed this silly non-code to stop; they needed to make some kind of legitimate arrangement. He had activities and spots to go to, and the molasses-moderate advancement they were making was driving him crazy.

He found the spot where he'd been before he'd left his position. He flattened himself as nearby to the sand as feasible, and slowly dogpaddled his way throughout the meadow possibly thirty yards between him and the building, and at least ten minutes in full view of anyone taking notice.

It took forever.

He qualified like a first-time stripper in a club brimming with lustful men. He believed he could intuitively detect anyone watching, but that was a fallacy; every little move he made professionally like a thunderous and obvious action that everyone inside could notice and hear no less anyone outside.

Interminable.

Be that as it may, he made it securely and Jackson pulled up nearby him, directly beneath the biggest pane on the rear of the structure. He could, without much of a stretch, hear them talking currently. Still difficult to identify precisely what they were stating in view of the muted voices and the acoustics or the language they talked made it unthinkable. Like shooting yourself in the back.

They lay there for a couple of minutes to make sure they hadn't been detected.

He took a look at Jackson as though to state, 'what now?' He scrunched his shoulders clearly not having any thoughts either way.

Why had they arrived this far? They wanted to know who was here, conceivably catch a few glimpses of them for future identification, but none of these were possible.

They weren't trying to make this simple on them. No one inside had any motivation to stare outside and they wouldn't need that in any case. They weren't that inconspicuous.

If they'd opened the aperture above them, it would've helped, though that would have gotten the two of them into the demonstration.

Without hesitation and given they were clearly outnumbered, he took a cavernous breath. They both turned and as silently as possible edged their way back to the forest and headed quickly back to the car.

Francis felt like a deserter, and that he'd let Cassie down.

Harbingers of danger and guilt, they arrived back at Francis's condo with neither the worse for wear except failure. Be that as it may, the roads had been cleared with no ice, and driving was a breeze. He made his way through town unabated and pulled up in front of Cassie's home area and parked.

Arriving, he decided to wait a few seconds to let his heart stop pounding as he struggled to imagine what she maybe could be wearing. Or not wearing. Their second day date had been right, encompassing seven daylights the primary one. He trusted she didn't pay attention to the fresh youngster's whiskers he'd chosen to let develop, assuming that a portion of his wounds may in any case appear, encompassing his jaw and the facial hair securing that zone of his mask pleasantly.

Taking a peek at himself in the rearview reflection verified even in the diminished glow originating her home, he appeared to be satisfactory, predominantly given the show hour she'd seen him.

Besides warning himself looks aren't everything, perhaps he appeared rough now. That means everything, doesn't it?

Francis knew she likely wouldn't be home. That the lights had stayed on during the day waiting for her not to return. And for that, he knew she was still lost in the darkest hour of the night without him knowing anything about where she was.

Yes, he considered what they might talk about were she to be here He wasn't sure she'd be keen about his evening session with his graduate understudies.

Maybe they could talk about her for a change, less about her family and more about her.

Appeared like a respectable idea. After all, who doesn't like to talk about themselves.

Gathering his wits, he headed for her front door. Couldn't believe how excited he was to see her. Perhaps to kiss again. If nothing else to stare at her.

Beautiful.

He knocked twice and waited.

No immediate answer.

Possibly she was still in the shower.

He knocked again, this time with the 'hello' tat-tat indication of recognition.

Why not?

They realized one another and it was a well-disposed knock.

But no answer.

The lights were on, so he rang the doorbell and heard it echo throughout the house and waited.

In any case, no answer.

Again, he rang the doorbell and heard its reverberation all through the house and paused. Again, no answer. Had she overlooked it?

Weird to envision she'd just lost track.

Again, no answer.

At that point, it jumped out at him. Cassie had been kidnapped.

He struggled with the door. Forward of him, but regardless, it appeared the best activity in the glow of the current situation.

Locked.

Doubly secured actuality for the handle gave a little and he could feel the deadbolt above it holding forward.

Did that mean she was home or she'd left by the back door? Possibly she'd altered her perspective on their relationship and didn't need to let him know. Was she covering up some point trusting he'd leave?

Given his life generally, he wouldn't accuse her. Exciting, but nonetheless risky. Not for the gloomy of heart.

He strolled about the house to the lawn. No fence. North Dakota was not big on fences. Maybe out in the farm lands to keep the swarm in, though certainly not in the urban areas or towns. Mostly not college towns. Who were you keeping out?

The back access was also locked.

He knocked twice on the door. No answer.

Getting nowhere. Feasibly, she was stuck at the market or someplace else. He could generally envision it so.

She would arrive home bearing gifts of meat and potatoes for the dinner they'd share in her dining room after which they'd sit in her living room and neck.

Neck. Still using that word these days?

He roamed around to the front of her house again, wondering if he should try to unearth a nosy neighbor to notice if any one of them had an idea where she could be.

Regrettably the houses on both sides of hers seemed dark at the moment. No lights in the after-hours. Zilch to show somebody staring at the TV or perusing by candlelight. No smoke from the chimneys.

Francis wished he had a working cellphone.

He got back in the Buick and drove toward town to find a phone to call her. Perchance she was back by now, or he could report her missing to the police. Would Patton trust him after their shenanigans this evening. Most of the daylight businesses had shut down so he killed two birds with one stone and drove directly to the police station. Patton wasn't in.

At first, he envisioned him still at the stockroom chipping away at fingerprints or whatever authorities did when they found the abandoned areas of offenders.

Francis then borrowed a phone against one of the desks and dialed Cassie's house. He remembered her number.

No answer.

He let it ring past as far as conceivable to end the call, yet still no answer. He could hear Patton telling him 'so what. She's probably escaped town by now, fearing your next bumbling efforts to solve the city's crimes.'

He gave a concerned citizen's report to the front desk clerk and made sure she wrote it down correctly. He signed it, and informed her it was an emergency; one-more person had vanished recently and no one had heard against her acknowledging. They shouldn't let that happen again.

She was very careful with the report and informed him the chief would get it first thing upon his return. He watched her cross the room and place it face up on Patton's desk.

Later he altered his depression and walked across the access.

He left the superstructure and drove the car in the direction Jackson had gone earlier that night.

He adjusted the lights on high and attempted to recollect the separations of various streets they'd passed as well as taken. Shouldn't name one of them also advertised for that. Both suddenly and now.

But before long, he'd at least found the turn on which the warehouse stood at the end of a long suddenly dark driveway and hoped he wouldn't miss it. Unfortunately, he passed the road and had to make a U-turn. He raced down the washboard earth until he saw the building straight ahead.

Seeing no motivation to make his quality a mystery, he drove directly into the glade and halted at the façade way to the spot. The lights internal were on and several uniformed cops ambled in and out like it was a routine daytime at Macys.

He got out of the rental and headed for the door. Lots of humans except them. Everyone looked busy doing everything but find Cassie.

CHAPTER 5.

A segment of white light spirited from the thirteenth floor, where a gathering of men and one lady forecasted his landing. Weird. It ought not to be lit given that there were no windows on that floor looking out from within. Perhaps it had some kind of separate mote-like outer passageway for the guards to keep what's within, within.

Francis remained in the parking garage gazing up at the structure trusting that somebody would instruct him. He recognized he needed to head within and then take the lift up to that thirteenth floor, nonetheless what anyone at that point intended. There, he should find Cassie, somehow kidnapped by CM—AKA Christopher Masters—if he hadn't murdered her yet.

The initial opportunity Francis emanated here he'd voyaged right from North Dakota. Ten hours on planes, transports, and cabs. Plenty of time to think. Yet nobody had jumped out at him those months prior.

The first opportunity he had, he'd run to Woodbridge, Connecticut; closer, yet he was similarly as befuddled then as at this new point. The hour he needed to accomplish something.

An adjacent interstate murmured with traffic that fed constantly the city that never rests. Yet the avenues closer about him were totally tranquil, as though the corridors of the city associated only with different urban communities, and left those of them in route unaware of what's pushing on.

He wondered about whether a low-flying plane might confuse the flickering red light as another plane and furrow under it, straightforward into the building. But the sky was vacant of airships aside from originating high-flying intercontinental flights taking travelers to Venice, Rome, or other common ports.

He envisioned himself there, endeavoring to communicate in Italian and getting a charge out of the gelato.

But all this was getting him nowhere.

He was due on that thirteenth floor in less than ten minutes and still had no reasonable or, for that matter, unreasonable plan. Perchance it was because he couldn't fathom what lay beyond the access. Seeing Cassie again.

He hoped to actually enable her with his ability in a military craftsmanship known as Bokator.

No risk he'd leave that apartment breathing, he assumed, but nonetheless he needed to take his risks. Otherwise Cassie wouldn't leave the room.

He remembered back to the hours in which it began. A not all that midyear like eve a couple of months past when the ice tripped him. He'd had guests in a little institute town in northern North Dakota where he instructed and inquired about and lived. Sometime in February, he thought.

Blaming his current predicament on anything other than his choice of examination topics would be convenient, but a lie. He knew what put him in the crosshairs and so did those like Cassie, who willingly understood the risks and yet stayed with him nonetheless.

He'd picked a fake name as an exploration subject, and calling had no suspicion. When he'd heard of the excitement, it would be caused on grounds and between web-based social networking and crackpots by the crowds in gatherings. What an existence.

Artificial life is the investigation of how to make living PCs. What had in-process become a kind of novelty, soon grew into elements far beyond his ability to control them. Requests for interviews and speaking engagements at other universities seemed insatiable. He was hooked not only on his apparent success, but bizarre as it may seem, his apparent lack of it as well.

He had now worked for years and garnered naught much so far except a maximum of attention for a minimum of solved goals. But he kept trying, because he was interested in how life came to be and whether or not he could turn the tables on whatever triggered it by creating it himself. Again, in machines.

Frolic God.

Why not?

Though God needn't be too worried, for Francis hadn't even come close.

One concern he had without hesitation, he'd entered the period of media study and bit the goad. That, therefore, had earned him a few solicitations every year to enter the clouded side of reproduction, which at that point drove him into driving others without wanting to go along with him in his endeavors. All of these—yes, every one of them—inconsequential, yet unavoidable. Welcome to Francis's world.

Damn cold. So, he made his way to the medication store and the telephone stall as quick-thinking as possible.

Once innermost, he hauled out the move of bills given him in return for a firearm, and acknowledged two things. First, he held ten tens, or a hundred dollars. Far more than the gun had probably been worth. Second, he stared at the phones in phone booths and noticed they did not take bills. He needed some change. That implied strolling to the counter and requesting transformation from somebody who might have been given a photograph and advised to tell the police or military in the event that they'd come and arrest him. In any case he had no way out.

But he strolled to the counter where an old money register sat by a melancholy looking young man perusing a comic book.

Francis inquired as to whether the young man could give him transformation for a ten. He protested everything without taking a peek at him. At that point, he rang the ringer on the register and stuffed the ten into a space, right one or not, and hauled his head out of the comics sufficiently long enough to give him four quarters, four ones, and a five. During all this, he didn't look at Francis once.

Ah, the joys of youth.

He returned to the corner, dialed the operator, and gave her Cassie's number, whereupon the operator reported he would need to place five dollars in quarters in the opening so as to connect.

This would give him one minute's time to talk including the rings it took to get her to the phone on the other end.

At that point, he walked back across the room and requested five-dollar's-worth of quarters.

The youngster still didn't turn toward Francis, only let out a burp, an unfathomable four-letter word, and started scooping out his register's quarters.

When he made it back to the corner, an additional person had taken his spot, awareness like he was in a Laurel and Hardy film, and sat on a chair next to the booth, obviously put there for that purpose, and waited his turn.

The store was doing a pretty spritely business for nighttime in a medium-sized town. The youngster was hardly able to keep his concentration moving in his comic book which he now noticed was a recent version of *Archie*. It apparently had extended publishing during his own childhood, and lived on as a relic of the American past.

The man in the stall hung up, and Francis immediately filled his space before someone else got the plan to utilize it.

Francis gave the operator the sum but got the same spiel he had the first time, and pushed in the quarters as quickly as he could.

He scanned his watch and waited for the connection.

The instant hand was at ten after, and his single second had begun.

The phone rang on the other end. Once. Twice. Three times. Ten seconds gone.

'Answer it, Cassie,' he whispered, too little boisterousness evidently even for an elderly person to gaze into the booth.

He finally hung up the phone when a dial tone replaced the sound of Cassie's voice that never fulfilled his dream.

CHAPTER 6.

Francis would have pulled out his laptop and looked through the Internet on his guests, had he anything to scan for. Joe was the main real name they'd given him. He was the lawful advocate.

What number of legitimate consultants in the country were named Joe? He didn't need to contemplate it. Fifty million dollars showed up effectively and appeared differently in relation to the concession he'd gotten for his exploration over the prior decade.

Be that as it may, at what cost would this help come. Doubtlessly he'd lose his reliability. Likely lose his psychological sufficiency worrying over spending a staggering leftover portion in prison. Who acknowledged what else?

He wouldn't do it.

Couldn't do it.

Go to damnation and forget about it, he let himself know. What's more, he did. He went to his bed. He didn't snooze unendingly.

What to do? Go to Patton, disappear near him, and ask him what happened? Whether or not he could find these people, they'd deny it. Indeed, even on the hazard that he edified them concerning the cost to PC customers, what perhaps could that prove? They hadn't really practiced any worry to devise an arrangement.

Was there a law against that?

After all, Francis didn't know their names, simply uncertain depictions.

Patton had a modest community police power and Francis bunches of understudies doing idiotic work. Taking lots of cop-hours.

Conceivably, he could go to the local reporters. Make a better than average story. Maybe he could get got by the wire administrators. At the point when it was out there, what could his guests do? He had no idea of their character. That wouldn't make the paper editors cheery. The sum total of what he had was a flawless little plot brought about by a clog of three men to make billions of dollars by beginning spreading a PC infection that would not really hurt any PC, simply make its client frantic as a hornet for a chance and they'd fix it so it wouldn't happen again for ten bucks a pop. Like a school stunt.

Be that as it may, it could make them a fortune numerous times over.

Unendingly he went endeavoring one potential course of action after another. Every open door he accepted, he had component but no karma. His guests had set this problem up carefully, he'd give them that.

Was he the man they really required?

Presumably.

Would it work?

Most likely.

Did he need the cash for his exploration?

Indeed.

Did it hurt anyone?

Truly. To a degree in any event. Not unending really.

No further to a decision than when he'd begun.

At three in the morning, he decided to change his insights to the love of his life, Cassie Davies, their school town's head overseer, and his own real sentiment.

Other than Patton and Jackson, an associate of his in the brain research division, she was the main person he trusted absolutely. A perfect fix to his stream issue sped up by his trio of visitors.

Past the point now where it was possible to call her and yet mulling over her was unwinding. Or, then again, imagining her alive and well, stimulated him in a way exceptionally but not equivalent to that which was moreover keeping him alert.

He took a few resting pills he'd set aside for such an occasion, and gestured into a fantasy of Cassie. A fantasy that centered in his mind alone, thank you very much.

He previously accepted it was ten-thirty in the AM and that he'd be followed for his top notch of the mind. That is in the event that he had one.

It was Saturday.

So, he lay in his bed and attempted to review Friday sunlight and watch it bounce back to him. The two mean folks. Patton. What's more, the three folks with the recommendation. Ten minutes. Generally. That is all it had taken.

He accepted his open door to the shower, cut his facial hair, and made breakfast or whatever he liked to call it. Espresso principally, and afterward eggs and toast.

He opened his door, still eating to begin the day right.

The kitchen window had given him a look at a cloudy sky, yet no snowflakes falling that he could see. Cold beyond question, but safe.

He didn't have a vehicle, so he sauntered everywhere on foot. That could be precarious given the climate, however having a vehicle didn't make things a lot simpler. He could consistently walk where others wouldn't drive.

Took longer. Sometimes. Sometimes not.

Further secure than endeavoring to surf on the as often as not cold and dangerous avenues.

He called Cassie again on the landline to hear her point of view of what his Friday brilliance maybe could mean.

She routinely had bits of information that sidestepped him.

She didn't answer after twelve rings. Most likely out for a walk or visiting a friend. While most people would consider their climate a difficulty, North Dakotans notice light like this as normal. Indeed, even commendable. Ideal for taking the pooch out to incorporate two or three fragrances or shopping.

Then Francis began to doubt his sanity.

Where was Cassie?

Really?

Regardless of his odds for success, but needing to confirm his e-mail anyway, he sat down at his home laptop and opened it to the Internet doing a quick confirm through his fresh message arrivals. As usual, it included a few stale invitations to conferences he would eventually turn down, lots of junk mail, and little else of interest.

In the primary gathering, an element emerged. He may have nibbled on one of them had they been putting forth to him not just repayment for costs regardless of the expense, yet an honorarium also. Perchance, even toss in an honor or two if only for his pride and remaining before a huge group as though he understood what he was saying.

The second gathering started with a title expressing locating your deluge without utilizing words! It grabbed his eye as proposed, and he opened it as somebody clearly needed and read the principal line. As was his typical habit, he caught the word *webinar* as if it had been thrown to him, and immediately forgot the rest of the message. He hadn't seen the word before, but quickly caught its meaning—a cross between seminar and web. Clever. Later, though, he temporarily disregarded his purpose in consulting the net in the first place.

As he remembered his thinking, he understood the sadness of coordinating living countenances with photographs of those appearances on his PC screen, and surrendered that pursuit before it abandoned him.

He called Cassie again and let it ring madly that she didn't have an answering machine. Something head librarians should have. No reaction.

Next, he phoned his department chair at home because it was Saturday. He replied and said he was sorry. At that point, he proved to ensure the tale about his classes journey secured was right.

He confirmed it.

What now? Any other call he made could be interpreted as him breaking a promise. Would also be something his three visitors perhaps couldn't anticipate his doing, and if they had his phone tapped would make good on their threat.

He had no suspicion what was happening. Initially the attack. Suddenly his visitors. That pursued by an offer he couldn't refuse.

And now he was rolling to leave his supposedly safe condo to visit the city. No genuine subtleties of anything beside a plot.

He believed calling Jackson, telling him of his plight, and asking him to rattle his psychologically addled intellect to emanate up with some kind of alternative. Tell him what he should be thinking about.

All he'd do, however, is pose inquiries and forecast that he should evaluate some speedy answers himself. Or priggishly disclose to him the appropriate responses were clear and what a schmuck he was for not making sense of them.

Rather he started pressing his fundamentals in as little a bag as he could discover. A duffle pack increasingly like it. Everything to take with him almost anywhere and not slow him down. Acknowledge he figured it was winter in a city like in North Dakota and he'd be wearing overwhelming garments to keep warm.

A few toiletries, his laptop, and several pocketbooks to keep him busy during bus rides, flights, taxies, and long waits at airports. He included a couple of packs of peanuts as snacks to be safe, and was then as organized as he was consistently going to be.

Neighboring four toward the evening the telephone rang. His as yet throbbing brain about completed a somersault to get to it before it rang once further.

CHAPTER 7.

When Jackson dropped Francis back at his home base encompassing midnight, Francis cautiously approached his condo. He had no inkling at that point who or what possibly could be waiting there for him.

The police had two plans for guards. But no one materialized, and after setting the alarm for four in the morning, Francis put himself into his bed.

His ride left at six and he required a chance to confirm his waking, get dressed, gobble a brief breakfast, and walk over to the station.

To get his mind into spending his next day of travel and what he seemed destined to do, he provoked his attention into thinking about anything different but related to place him at rest. That isn't the same to artificial life by having zilch explicitly to do with science, yet adhered to by consistent presence.

This night he picked anything to be explicit; the originating of the universe. What if, for example, black holes were responsible for those harbors familiarly at the centers of galaxies that can't be seen, but which ravage through mammoth gravity attraction to gather up stars, nebula, and planets before heading out on their own to scavenge other likely universal matters to feed upon.

His diversion this nightfall, was to study if the big bang—our big bang for example—hadn't begun being such a hopeless drifter, and in so thinking spanned different hard-to-react-to questions that continued pestering cosmologists about their extreme issues in the world.

For example, it at least partially solved the question of what happened before their singular Big Bang, the answer living within the zillions of gloomy holes against a multiverse of such in various states of existence. It answered the whole confused notion of infinity, the solution being there was no time before the future and no hours after that opportunity either. Simply place the universe as going on forever having opportunity and space and it had always been that way.

As good as his self-indulged solution to these paradoxes seemed to be, his attention kept returning to his current situation. He was going to pull up stakes and flood quick to one of the universe's greatest urban regions and, at any rate, guarantee to spurn his regard by appealing himself with a corrupt endeavor that at whatever point gotten, could visit him in the hoosegow or pokey for a fortnight of weeks, months, or even years. All of which, for the assurance of assumed permit money, would reinforce his investigative work identifying with artificial life. After all, in his work to avoid it he found himself right back at square one—sleepless and frustrated as the hours tiptoed by, departing him once again, right where he had initiated.

By three in the morning, he'd get and attend a dream-world social event, his stuff and drinking a pot overflowing with coffee, believing later when it was laying on the vehicles or airplanes he would take or be taking catnaps in the taxicabs, or whatever else he wound up riding in for diminutive outings. It would make his nights into day and a different way that. His life would continue in light of the way that they required it. And that's when he faltered, slumbering only to be roused in an hour or so by his alarm clock.

Living.

The minute he finished locking his vanguard entryway subsequently that next day, he could feel someone watching him. This wasn't fear, just that delicate tendency on the back of his neck.

He realized someone was out there.

Didn't know how he knew it, but he did.

Snow had proceeded falling leisurely from the mist above a sign of another nice day. Real storms either began as blizzards or high winds or both.

Casually passing fronts made the flakes come down few and far between.

In all likelihood, he pushed for exceptional sunshine and long walks shopping or driving some place. What he would do.

Or not.

Not.

He'd take a bus south to Bismarck. Later, a diminutive flight from there to Fargo. From there, he'd fly to midway in Chicago, get a taxi transversely over town to O'Hare, and starting there on to the tremendous city. Not that Chicago wasn't a big city, it was, though naught quite aims to please as the Big Apple does.

Decisively, then, next a taxi to his certified objective.

The whole trip would take about ten hours. Minus the two-hour difference in hour zones then, he'd arrive just after rush hour. Wonderful.

The disguised eyes followed him appropriately to the cab station.

Apparently meant to watch him instead of cause issues.

He arrived alive and still perfectly healthy. Beside the bus driver and the woman taking tickets, he was the only one in the place. Ten minutes before departure, he found a seat up front on the otherwise empty bus, so if the weather altered and it took them longer than projected, he'd be the primary one off. He could've sat in the back row for all the difference it made.

Just him and the driver.

All the way to Bismarck.

Winter with delicately falling snow, sleet, ice, snowflakes. and hail. Benevolent and what fun.

He misplaced eyes faster or last-minute before he entered the vehicle station so it ceased to be an issue.

The driver may have been a talker anyway over the bustle the diesel engine made, but he couldn't have heard him at any rate. So, he sat back and rested his eyes, hoping he'd gauged the rest of his way there correctly.

No such luck. The roaring solid of the motor and the occasional burp of the exhaust guaranteed that.

Feasibly, he'd compensated for wasting time with some reading. About PC diseases. He realized all the basics, but hackers were upping the odds of success every day. Finding out the most ebb and flow, little-known systems couldn't hurt him paying such little awareness as to how things altered where he was going.

The articles didn't discuss him or allude to his work in their arrangements of sources. Wasn't without question whether that satisfied him or gave him melancholy.

Occasionally, he stared out the pane at the barren meadows, pastures, and fields they passed.

Covered in cavernous hail, endless of which would remain throughout the winter. Probably could sink a pipe into it, pull out a sample, remove it from the pipe, and observe concern akin to the cliffs of the Grand Canyon time scales, measured in weeks and months instead of centuries.

An on-coming car whizzed by them once every fifteen minutes or so. Not pitiful. Just alone. A big difference.

He appreciated this spot. The Missouri river cut through Bismarck, though it didn't cross it considering the municipal airport lies out of town to the east.

The hail had ceased falling and patches of brilliance appeared here and there over the flat landscape. Encompassing ten in the initial segment of the day. Possibly they'd have lookouts waiting for him here as well.

They did.

From the moment he stepped out of the bus door, he could feel the eyes again. Not comparable ones he suspected, but eyes regardless. Interested in him.

In any case, he had thirty minutes to keep things under control for his plane. This hour, a gathering had surrounded the on outside stairs.

'All aboard for Fargo,' he thought.

They'd caused a slow crawl into civilization. Men and women dressed for white-collar businesses. A few farmers all the more of them. A few pilots flying as voyagers to get one-more flight they'd be coordinating without vulnerability.

Some eyes looking at the back of his neck had vanished, but they could be taking the trek with him. He'd never know definitely, for they realized accurately where he was seated and where he was going.

No inspiration to look.

Next it was an hour to charge for the cabs and trying to make his departure from O'Hare. Unlike his seatmate on the plane, the cab driver kept noiseless during their diminutive ride.

When they arrived quicker than required by later afternoon traffic, he tipped him well. At that point, he made his association and got a satisfyingly calm seat for the final leg of the flight. No opportunity for paranoia, just a snooze.

They arrived at Kennedy in the early night. They could notice the stars above beginning their vigil. Only three or four of them given the lights of the city, but stars nonetheless.

Francis found a cab and gave him the house, and off they went, his journey practically over. What a day.

As they drove through the city, he pondered what he would do about the circumstance he'd ended up in. The devious plan his captors had rigged for him actually had some merit. Their methodology emerged to be consistent with his Achilles heel to keep him in line.

Cassie.

But could or would he go through with it? No way. Though how could he avoid it?

Fortunately, they absolutely had no idea what he did, so perchance he could pull all manner of tricks to mystify and confuse them. After all, they'd explained him as no one of merit, and that could compete with his knowledge of the subject. Regardless, he figured a ten-year old could do what they needed. But what did he know?

His goal was a tall structure with a solitary red luminosity on top, squinting in the evening sky like a cyclops.

He paid the driver and included a huge tip.

Why not? Wasn't his money.

And there he stood. Waiting. For what?

He gazed concerning the huge glass entryways and the lit name above them. As if that explained everything. Like what they did here.

Lawyers, bankers, candlestick-makers. The diminished glow appearing through the glass sheets implied the structure was shut for the evening.

Great.

All this way and him standing in vanguard of a vacant construction on the outskirts of New York City with elements to do, nowhere to go, and without a cellphone.

Then he noticed a figure motivating neighboring in the shadows at the rear of the large entranceway trailing the doors. Glass doors. Likely a nightfall watchman.

No harm in trying, so he rapped softly on the glass hoping to catch his attention.

No response.

He tapped, once added. Harder this time.

It worked.

The figure sauntered gradually over the space toward him. Deliberately, as though suspicious he may prepare to storm the bastille for every one of the treats central. Choice example.

All he could think of was Cassie.

Where was she?

Really?

CHAPTER 8.

Francis thought of Cassie. Did she miss him? Why hadn't she called? Had she informed her sibling Patton? Were the police making requests? Was it snowing in North Dakota? Was he actually as big an idiot as he was demonstrating himself to be?

He chose out of the blue that he could examine to stare through his temporary condo. There must be one more way to the outside universe of corridors and lifts, else how could whoever was conveying his suppers get them in there?

But as impossible as it seemed, he wouldn't find a single sign of one. Feasibly entire walls opened electronically with a whoosh, like in *Star Trek* on the *Enterprise*. Or the cook crept out underneath the pantry sink or the latrine. He even peeked beneath the bedstead to observe if someone perhaps could be hiding there.

No to everything.

The lab and his apartment had been painted the same drab hue. No art on the walls. In fact, naught on the walls at all. That was probably an inkling, though he couldn't study a sign as to what.

No lights or different neon signs he could see. The dividers and roof sparkled with an iridescence that served to enlighten the rooms. Never faltered or turned evening black. A bizarre quality of zoo. He ran his hands over the walls originating corner to corner. No expulsions of any character. No scars that would give away some character of concealed entryways.

Someone had gone to incredible inconvenience in structuring this spot. To keep individuals central and all over sustained while appropriately urged to work. Exhausted against his sci-fi surroundings, he hit the hay and urged himself to rest. No go. For the first time the constant light bothered him as well as the lack of any sound except a very low hum. Probably the supercomputer cooling system.

The whole area gave him the willies.

And claustrophobic.

Caged in.

Nowhere to go.

When he woke, he wasn't sure he'd relaxed or lay in a half sleep for several hours. Didn't matter a lot, though, as he didn't feel tired.

But he'd drink some espresso and in any case gobble a bit of buttered toast and stay put for the day to monitor whether he could get whoever it was that readied the sustenance and discover how they got into his galley.

Decided against it. Not in his nature to waste time.

Once in the main room Cassandra (not Cassie) and he conversed in tongues. It must have appeared like seventy percent or so of what they said had little or no obvious meanings. He actually couldn't have recollected his lines if someone cavorted them back to him. Probably make for an extraordinary out deafening Rorschach test. Their coded conversations covered only those areas they qualified necessary to keep secrets. In other words, at least for him, how the hell to get out of Dodge.

Cassandra was as yet hesitant. Could be they were straightforward and would pay her like her different customers had. Bigger stakes. But she, in the long run, gave in.

Again, using their code, she asked him how they could do it. With that she had him stumped. The only way he could identify it, was for him to take the head man out on his next visit, and make for the exits.

Pretty full the hour he had her persuaded, the entryway opened, and in sauntered the cookie monster. CM. Christopher Masters. Whatever.

Without advice, he handed him a knife-hand strike directly to the jugular, catching the third vertebra of his spinal column in the process. Down he went. He'd be out for at any rate twelve hours. Except for an awful cerebral pain, he'd be fine generally.

Cassandra opened her mouth, assumed better of whatever she was expecting to say, and we went out the door and to the right. As great a bearing as any other.

Francis invested his energy amid lunch, gazing at each square centimeter of obvious dividers, and roof space in the pantry. Not much.

The floor was tile. Problematic to tell where an entryway may shroud given every one of the spaces between tiles loaded up with grout and those immovably set. Solid as rock.

Anything everyday he could identify there.

He professed to search for something under the sink, but regardless researched the floor instead. Cement. He knocked on it to make sure the apparent hard surface was real. It was. No way could a concealed entryway cover up there.

Getting once added into his seat to complete his lunch, he peeked about yet again. A microwave. Not sufficiently large for anybody to slither into or out of. An icebox brimming with crisp nourishment. False backing. He checked pretending to get added relish for his sandwich. No go. A stove. He turned on a burner. It worked. Looked in the oven. A genuine stove. Not a chance. A storage room resembling a plausibility, yet when he researched it—in the wake of claiming to drop a morsel and obviously looking for a sweeper to tidy it up—he found a genuine storeroom with a strong solid genuine floor evidently the constitution of the whole division between him and the space beneath.

We were on the thirteenth floor, the one most modelers let well enough alone for their outlines; however, this one they'd some way or one more left in.

But what difference did that make? What would a thirteenth floor of a superstructure have that any other floor wouldn't have as well? Nothing he could study except if misfortune looked like an entryway.

Tormented by his absence of advancement, he completed his sandwich and put its remains in the sink.

Soon-after he got an idea. Not loads of one, but why not.

He scrounged around in his pockets for a slip of paper, found one and jotted a note of thanks to his invisible and probably non-existent cook and bottle washer. Possibly he'd learned the concept. What, he had no clue.

He rejoined Cassandra in the prison they called a workplace, and set about to build the precious antivirus that would make their virus impotent.

The entire believe materialized as living crazy. Initial primary forms that completed a specific element, and after that manufacture one more anything to debilitate it.

After that they'd rake in their dough. He'd have to incorporate everything, all of everything in his code to ensure these concepts didn't occur. Unfortunately, that would most likely just stall the process. So perhaps create elements to prevent them from figuring out what he'd finished before it went to market. After that, he'd reveal their intent to the world, as they were hauled away to court and afterward jail.

He stared at Cassandra occasionally. Maybe to aid him to find Cassie. She never thought back, nonetheless merely furrowed her forehead in a practically hyper route with whatever she was doing at the time.

Buried in her computer screen, and likely revved up and ready to go. That's when motivation hit. Where the cameras and microphones were hidden. Every monitor in the spot had one of each. Obvious. In fact, so obvious he would never have thought of it had he not wandered his eyes concerning Cassandra.

He developed inquisitively about what feasibly could occur on the gamble that they pointed their screens straightforwardly at each other.

Criticism. Like endless mirrors reflecting ever smaller images of themselves in hotel rooms that have mirrors on opposite sides of the bathroom sink. The visual images probably wouldn't represent an issue, yet the sound may work to an emergency point that could demonstrate fascinating results. But to what end?

Concern might change, but time will certainly continue forward. And perhaps his mental stability. He rebounded to work, realizing that his guardians could stare straightforwardly into his eyeballs as he'd done. No assistance for his focus. In the meantime, he was satisfied to have a house of another of those numerous baffling inquiries that went up against him.

That evening, if that was the thing that passed rapidly, and before he cogitated it daily he had roughed out a variant of the antivirus with nothing left but to test and retest it, and after that work with Cassandra to finish the bundle.

He bid her goodnight and rebounded to his apartment.

Not long after he'd shut the entryway, he heard a delicate yet persistent knock.

Who'd knock? The entryway had no lock. In fact, he'd come in to shield himself. He opened the entryway. As soon as he did, it pushed fully accessible and Cassandra (not Cassie) leaped into his arms. Literally.

CHAPTER 9.

Francis remembered back to a time when Jackson, Cassie, and he made a terrible set of mistakes that gave all three a sense of adventure that they'd never forget. A true nightmare that could have ended deadly if it were not for the luck of the Irish. It might have been worse had not they all survived the barrage of bullets and especially the complete lack of evidence of anything but terror.

Cassie and Francis had taken a brief vacation, had cleaned up, and visited the restaurant in the motel for a late dinner. A rainstorm had initiated in earnest and they wanted to brave the weather to take a chance on another greasy spoon. Still a bad choice. A plain cheeseburger would have likely tasted good in comparison. But none offered on the menu.

Back in their room, Cassie studied the map for possible side trips into the mountains the next day, while Francis spent time studying Cassie.

Sometime around ten, Francis heard what sounded like a car backfire. Cassie asked if he'd heard it. Francis nodded and waited for something to follow. Nothing else.

She eventually shrugged her shoulders and went back to studying her maps, but the second backfire really caught their attention. Cassie's look suggested a more 'what now?'

"That a backfire?"

Francis gave her his 'haven't-a-clue look, and they waited.

Silence.

And then all hell broke loose. The front door to the room, the one Francis realized too late he'd forgotten to lock, burst open followed quickly by a huge man whose muscles reminded him of Rasmussen.

The man slammed the door behind him and stared at the two of them. He was dripping wet and holding a large handgun which he brandished about like a drunken teacher might a pointer during a lecture.

"What?" he said to no one in particular. He was confused about something. Probably how easily he'd been able to enter the room.

Cassie then followed with 'what?'

The unexpected visitor leaned back against the closed door as if attempting to keep someone else from entering. Francis noticed the blossoming red splotch growing in the center of the man's chest. He wheezed out yet another 'what?'

Before he slid down the door to a sitting position on the floor, his slide leaving a red tread on the door, but this little scene was far from over.

Two more backfires sounded as two bullets burst through the room's front window. Since both Cassie and Francis were sitting on the floor, neither of these bullets came close to them, but it still proved unnerving.

Cassie, working on instinct, crawled in the direction of the uninvited guest, no doubt to offer medical aid.

Francis grabbed and pulled her back. This was no time for aiding and abetting a possible enemy. As if things hadn't degraded far enough, Francis heard sirens in the distance. Great! One more murder to nail him for. Why not? What difference will another one more or less make? They could only execute him once.

By this time their wounded visitor regained whatever consciousness he had left and pulled himself up using the door jam. He turned around sway from the two of them, and, still holding the gun, jerked the door open and fired four or five rounds blindly in the direction of the parking lot.

He must have hit something, for before he'd finished, someone below let out a bloodcurdling cry. The muscleman slammed the door shut again and reloaded his gun. He then found a new position against a wall rather than the door, a position saving him from being shot again as another bullet from outside hit the door and whizzed through the room finding a spot over the bed's headboard to enter the wall. Real bullets, as if anyone needed proof.

Cassie looked at him.

Using the sign language they'd adopted over the time they'd been together she asked Francis what to do. No idea.

"What do you want from us?" Cassie screamed in the direction of the man near the door.

He looked stunned for a second, as if he'd only just then become aware of their presence. Then he pulled the door open again and fired randomly several more times toward the same parking lot.

No one screamed this time. But no one fired back either.

The police had probably arrived.

Order finally.

Not the case. The visitor had slammed the door in time for a volley of bullets to pepper it as he stepped aside.

He looked at them again. Confused. The door behind him then literally came unhinged. Several men, all dressed in suits, crushed into the room backwards obviously facing others who had pushed them into retreat. These were the muscleman's men apparently.

Bullets whizzed above their heads. The men grabbed their wounded leader and headed for the back of the room. Behind them Francis could hear rushing footsteps coming toward the door. And behind them, the sirens continued to wail.

Now Francis could hear the voices of cops yelling instructions to their minions.

Grabbing Cassie's hand, Francis wrestled her into a lying position over which he placed his own body. Ever the graceful protector.

From there, Francis could see enough of the action to tell him the visitor's men had gotten the worst of the battle.

After a minute or two, Jackson began fighting his way back into Francis's life. He'd guessed he'd known he was still alive all along, though it was still a shock seeing him here, looking fit and ready for the action he seemed to love. With all these people in close proximity in such a small space, and with all parties except Cassie and Francis having guns, the casualties ran high. Bodies dropped this way and that. Francis doubted now anyone was actually winning, but maybe surviving meant victory.

The police gave chase up the outside staircase, their voices screaming 'stop in the name of the law!'

If anyone would know how to survive, it was him.

So, when he dashed for the bathroom, Francis grabbed Cassie and gave chase, having no idea the bathroom offered escape, but so be it. They probably should have waited for the police since they'd be in their hands shortly anyway. Somehow, though, running seemed the better choice at the moment.

When they reached the bathroom, Jackson turned toward the lone window above the shower and fired several times, stitching a line down toward the floor. Most of the plaster and mortar holding the upper wall together, then blew away.

Francis assumed this tactic involving so many gunshots would also deter the cops from entering the room behind them so quickly. Neither Cassie nor Francis could hear anything but the echoes of gunfire and the occasional roar of thunder from the storm outside.

As the smoke cleared the wall, it lost its battle against gravity and most of it crumbled away. How Jackson planned to escape, through, eluded him. They were on the second floor and though Francis realized he had rock climbing experience, scaling down sheer flat walls with no handholds would be challenging.

As the cops crashed into the body-filled room behind them, they stopped firing. At that second, Jackson launched himself through the opening he'd made in the wall without any apparent regard for where he'd land on the other side.

Cassie gave Francis one of those looks, as if to say, 'all right dweeb, what now?' Grabbing Cassie's hand and out they went into the cold and wet darkness, where to land nobody, least of all Francis, knew. Certainly expecting a fairly long journey into night, it surprisingly wasn't what happened. As soon as they'd followed Jackson on his way to apparent freedom, they landed on terra firma. Actually, Francis landed on what he thought was terra, but wasn't.

Cassie landed on terra Jackson.

The second-floor room apparently turned into a first-floor room at the rear of the motel. Then Jackson rolled Francis off his back. He grunted some sort of expletive and attempted to run from the scene.

Without any simple alternative, Francis reached out, grabbed Jackson's ankle, and held on for dear life. It reminded him of grappling on the cliff face in Lee Vining Canyon once. In reverse.

Cassie, seeing Francis's ploy, reached for his ankle and held on for dear life too, as if their ankle's chain had some chance of succeeding.

It didn't.

Jackson shook his ankle loose from Francis's grip and took off in the direction of the parking lot. He reached back and grabbed Cassie. Together they followed him as fast as they could.

Apparently, Jackson thought the police in their haste had forgotten to leave anyone behind to protect their cars. If so, he'd been right.

As the two of them arrived at the lot, Jackson ran for the nearest police car and jumped in, revving the engine and burning rubber as he headed for the highway.

Francis had no idea what to do. So, his better half took over. Cassie pulled him into another police cruiser, took the driver's seat, and off they went chasing a wild man in their own stolen police car. Both cruisers had their roof lights flashing and as they entered the main drag, some of the populace still awake and in their cars at that hour, pulled off road to avoid their rampaging cars.

For once, Francis thought he was tailing someone and not being tailed himself. A good feeling, especially since he wasn't driving, but wrestling himself into the passenger-side seatbelt. Safety above all.

Francis held on and left Cassie to tear the hell out of the tires and brakes.

They slid their way toward the next small town north, without doubt for a second the chase would be short-lived. Police don't take kindly to having their cars stolen, especially after leaving a bloodbath the size of the one they'd left in their wake. Francis had no doubt they were even now gathering a multi-city task force to bring them in.

For the moment, though, it was grand fun. A car chase right out of Hollywood films. After all, as guilty as Cassie and Francis were, they were both innocent and somehow the truth would out.

Maybe.

The ride, though, was brief; for as quickly as they left the city limits, Jackson pulled someone over. Francis had to give the guy credit. He was at the height of his escape and apparently going to give someone a speeding ticket. What balls.

Cassie, who had pulled us to a stop as well, looked over at him.

"What? We can't stay here."

Francis recovered quickly.

"Let's go." Whereas he jumped out the door. With her yelling back and pointing toward the car that Jackson had now hijacked in which he was driving away.

Francis reached his passenger door, pulled it open, slid Cassie into the front seat, and forced himself in beside her.

"Hell, Francis, you're a damn pest." Jackson yelled and glared at him.

"Drive!" Francis actually felt like he belonged in this scene. Somehow, he'd caught up to the game and no longer had to apologize for being behind the eight-ball.

The rain turned to a downpour and the wipers could hardly keep the visibility clear enough to see the road. Lightning tore apart the night sky followed by enveloping roils of thunder.

The cops would have a hard time catching them in this mess, even when they got their act together enough to figure out what they'd done. He'd have to ditch this car eventually, but for now it would do fine.

They splashed through puddles the size of ponds and avoided other cars by passing them on the opposite side of the road.

"Where are we going?" Cassie screamed. Jackson answered, "Taking Francis here to the cops."

The wind whipped us back and forth across the highway. Most of the traffic, both oncoming and parallel, had stopped alongside the roadside. They, on the other hand floated serenely by having a pleasant mid-evening conversation about who was and who wasn't dead.

Cassie decided to give up. She lay back and began crying quietly. Francis had been in some dire straits in the past couple of weeks, but this one seemed different somehow.

He looked at Jackson. "What was all that about back there?"

"The muscleman? Had to put him out of his misery. Clean things up a little."

Francis wasn't sure that helped much, but it was better than nothing.

"Who was he?"

"Nobody of consequence. Someone with dough who wanted more of it. Paid your bail, though. I used him like I use everybody."

"If you used him for bail to get me out of jail, why are you taking me back there now? Makes no sense."

"I thought you'd lead me to something useful. All it did was get the muscleman more involved than he should have been. You're a trouble magnet, Francis. I need you somewhere safe a while longer."

Not sure he liked his tone.

"You're supposed to be dead."

"Never going to get it, are you, Francis?"

He smiled.

"I think there's a bunch of your lookalikes wandering around and when one of you gets killed another takes his place."

Actually sounded pretty reasonable given the circumstances.

"You wish."

"Why do I wish you'd not have to confront the fact that I am Jackson."

The rain had turned to a soft patter by this time as had the conversation. The storm passed going east and the driving became smoother.

The other cars on the road joined them again and they continued their way north.

Sometime later, Francis fell asleep.

When he woke, Cassie was dozing and Jackson still driving. The morning sun threw the cars' moving shadow toward the mountains to their left.

"Where are we?"

"Where do you want to be?"

Like talking to a damn Cheshire Cat.

He could see high desert signs advertising various businesses ahead.

With the question resolved, Cassie awoke.

"We need to make a pit stop," the driver announced.

"Breakfast, no?"

He ignored the question and parked in the lot of a strip mall, got out, and wandered into a clothing store just opening for the day.

They heard some rattling around inside for a moment.

Then Jackson came out and pointed at them to follow him. They got out of the car and did so.

'Why not?' Francis thought as he looked at the other cars parked in front of the store, picked one, and got in. He motioned for the two of them to join him. They did. Why not? He started the car and backed out of its parking space and off they went.

In yet another stolen car.

CHAPTER 10.

Eventually Francis made his way into the lab and found his station. Cassandra (not Cassie) was still buried in her work and didn't look up. For that he was grateful. He didn't want to hear any offhand comments she possibly could have about Cassie at the moment.

What to do? After all, if they were dead anyway, why not leave it be?

Transform nothing with the exception of the creation era, so he'd be upbeat at long last, keep his piece of the deal, and let everything else go. While he may be dead, at any rate he'd know he had to be brought down to get that way.

Of course, there was that minuscule possibility he'd keep his side of the deal. He couldn't perceive how, though it was the main way to make due aside from getting away and letting the world make its concept of its own fate. Maybe that was it.

He, at that point, began to go through again in this little snake eating its tail drama, with no genuine shot of busting the chain.

After a few hours of coding, not copious of any concern except giving whoever happened to be watching at the second, the logic that he was in fact working as promised allowed him to return to his apartment.

Cassie relaxed on the cot. Supper for two was obviously filled in as though the gourmet expert had perused his psyche. He hated to wake her, but after two bites of the lamb, he couldn't allow her to miss it.

With a couple of nibbles herself, she concurred. They drank a container of wine and ate the three courses as though they hadn't eaten a couple of days past. After an hour of this and not saying a word to one another, she gave him that look. He appreciated it, believed further than she'd ever know, but he peered apropos the ceiling indicating his hope there weren't prying eyes there. Did she feel great making whoopee before what possibly without a doubt drew a multitude of people from a crowd of grisly elderly men?

She then gave him the 'wait' scowl, realizing she'd disregarded the unwritten laws that pervaded their existence there.

With no concept to watch, hear, or read, they necked. In the kitchen. Neither of them needed to hazard the cot once further.

Eventually the chef's minions climbed up through the hole in the floor, took away the dishes, and cleaned up after themselves and them.

Cassie and he found the cot. For rest, not the something different that would have been their inclination.

Try as he might, though, he couldn't nap. Beyond tired. As far as he could recall, he hadn't dozed in practically twenty-four hours.

But no go.

He let his attention free associate. A little concept that his work in unreal intelligence had taught him. He gave himself the present bind as the issue, and afterward let the principles go, including outside the field of diversion.

When he'd finished, the only thing with countenance was anything that Cassandra had whispered to him when he last saw her.

"Get back in the game," she'd said. What had she implied with that remark? Why had it remained with him? Wasn't he officially back in the game?

He thought about it. No, really, he was not back in the game. He'd simply returned. She'd implied turning it into a functioning frolic. Or at least that's what he realized he wanted her to have said.

But what did that mean? What's more, when he had concern to genuinely study about and perhaps some quality of real sign, he fell asleep. Deeply dozing. And did not wake for many hours.

Cassie decisively rubbed his arm enough times to pull him out of a dream where Cassandra was trying to get him to give her another hit of the meth he'd bought her.

Suddenly meal and back to work. Same old drag. But he recollected his thoughts before he'd fallen asleep.

'Get back in the game.'

Conceivably, what he wanted her to say was get IN the game.

Some way or someone else that energized him. Not certain why.

He invested a lot of his energy gazing at computer screens while pondering what he would do, starting with a various leveled rundown of what was most significant, and what the least while an arrangement gradually developed. In his system, for example, it was constructed of three essential standards.

Primary and perhaps chief, Cassie's life could accurately compare to the universe's computers. He had no indication what crippling them would cause. It could mean millions would die in nuclear explosions. It could also mean we'd go back to a slower and simple time when humans retained to someone else in less chaotic ways. Screw the second law of thermodynamics.

Second, take the antivirus on a thumb drive, or as a memory in his concentration, and handicap the supercomputer in the lab so nobody but him could discharge it to the world. Place everything right.

Third, escape. The hardest part.

How could he be able to do it given the expanded security that Masters had no uncertainty set up cogitating his past effective 'rush-to-opportunity' through the passage in the storm cellar that evening such a long time ago. In any event he'd framed an arrangement that may work.

Cause in full disarray in the structure as he could, by releasing the infection on the supercomputer itself. Why hadn't he really thought about that previously? It had been invulnerable in light of the fact that it had no connection to the outside world. No entrance to the Internet, email, or any of the concern that they presently underestimate.

With the homegrown computer muddled by the random appearing windows, the central processing unit would begin to fail. He didn't realize that without hesitation, but he thought it would. In the turmoil that followed, he'd once again become the focus of everyone's attention. Exactly what he wanted. He needed to be in that room again with everyone involved around him. Not to work them out of their arrangement or their adoration for their president, yet to exhibit his Bokator aptitudes. Logic and bears be accursed. Once released, he could do a lot of harm. Not that he especially needed to hurt Masters' adherents, however he wanted to cause sufficient wreckage that his bureau would then be called upon to fix it. That's when he'd even the odds.

Soon after, he believed in the *coup de grace*. Plant a bomb. Tell them about it. Clear the building. Not a real bomb, only an alarm. Enough to work.

With the computer pushing haywire, it should be elementary to disappear, especially when they were too busy doing so many other concerns. He could likewise shave his facial hair. Make it harder for them to identify him. Dress Cassie one like Cassandra two.

Enough with the goal that they wouldn't be viewed as a danger. It could work. All of a sudden, he felt certain. He'd completed what Cassandra character three had recommended.

He'd make himself a genuine player. A functioning member, though he had no suspicion what Cassie and he would do once they got away. If they escaped. It absolutely wouldn't keep the cops off their backs, and it would make him progressively defenseless since without the facial hair he'd seem increasingly like the sequential executioner he'd been portrayed in the newspapers.

They'd also still be in the crosshairs of the competition, though he had less noticed them considering their apparent efforts at kidnapping him which had proven so idiotic. But you never know. Perchance they were keeping their real guns in the back room and would pull them out at the last minute to surprise him. What's higher, he wouldn't expel Masters and his groupies. They'd be mad as hornets without nests.

With every concept taken into account, still a decent arrangement. If everything worked, they'd be in a position of power, not of weakness.

He stressed though over Cassie. She was a librarian. A wonderful actor, yes, yet one who'd be awkward on the run. He wouldn't forgive himself for putting her in harm's way. Yet he wouldn't leave her either. He'd be right back at the starting block. He'd need to fill her in on the subtleties after he put his arrangement vigorously afterward instead of previously.

Obviously telling her with the cameras running, wouldn't be a decent thing, but he could try the same code he'd used with Cassandra, but wouldn't be sure she hadn't given that to Masters with everything else she'd ordered him to do. Getting his Cassie to follow the plan without knowing he had a plan was simply pushing to take to chance. Justified, despite all the trouble he figured. He could at least give her a heads up. No subtleties, just a basic recommendation to hang with him. In the long escape, he advanced into the lab and found his station.

CHAPTER 11.

Francis's initial inclination was to dump the vehicle. They'd stolen it, and he couldn't risk getting pulled over by a cop. It would just add a stolen vehicle and firearm to his record.

However, he'd rather not get captured so effectively as that. He hadn't worn gloves, so he tried to touch as few of everything as possible in order to clean what evidence he'd already left for them before abandoning the old crate.

Actually, he hated to give it up. Ran well, at least a lot better than it looked. But he imagined the owner was looking forward to getting it back in the same condition as he'd last seen it.

Francis was driving through a curious town of marginally typical and various soil streets, charging opposite to the primary drag. He picked one of these indiscriminately, and drove down it a mile or two.

Once there, he wiped the car clean and left it alongside the road. Looked fairly safe. Then he bolted leaving the keys inside by locking the door and holding the handle trigger as he shut it.

About four in the afternoon by now, with the sky clouding up, he needed a spot to stay and a meal only the latter of which he could afford at this point. That is, if the town had an extremely shoddy motel. Perhaps he could sell the firearm. Add some spice to the village gossip.

He strolled into town resembling an unshaven woods homeless person. No issue the townsfolk appeared occupied with planning for the big storm arriving soon. Logs heaped high in pickup beds and packs of street salt hauled in vehicle trunks just as original coats, journey purchased at garment stores. People were too busy to notice another denizen of the wilds walking the streets. Besides he'd hunkered down within the watchman's coat.

So far, he doubted anyone could detect him anyway.

The main motel he passed promoted fifty-dollar rooms to lease for the night. Appealing given the probable ice on its way though, but it would leave him with only a few bucks for meals and next he'd be broke.

Stealing guns was about as far as he'd go at this point. Shouldn't detect himself holding up a supermarket, regardless of how terrible anything got.

Toward the finish of a parkway, he ran over somewhere else. This one advertised rooms at thirty dollars an evening including dinner and continental breakfast. He took one peek at the sky and chose he'd better exploit it. No telling where they'd uncover him otherwise.

A solidified six-foot-tall popsicle took the outside mass of a coffee shop encompassing the local area. He went innermost to observe if they had a room at the inn.

The man behind the counter appeared perplexed when he asked about availability. Soon after he noticed why. Of the twenty or so mailboxes next to him, all had keys in them. Apparently not the best of choices. His decision. Picking a count aimlessly he gave him cash for one night and asked him when supper would be prepared. That caught the man short. Apparently not exclusively was the spot unfilled, yet it had been so for quite a while.

"Eight o'clock sharp," he finally stated.

He bobbled and let himself get back to whatever he needed to get back to and Francis found his room out back looking like the rest. An outhouse among outhouses.

He'd brought nothing aside taken his recently stolen weapon, and found the room had valuable little space notwithstanding for that. A bed, a bathroom without a shower, and several hundred bugs that ran for their holes in the walls when he turned on the light. Quite a vision.

He surmised he'd at last wound up in a sorry situation. But it did have a cot which he sorely needed at this point. So, he laid down on it. Or rather in it. The mattress had misplaced most of its giveback. Shockingly, it was delicate and with two or three hours left before supper, he shook off.

He woke to the sound of little critter feet charging across the floor, the breeze howling outside blowing snow through the cracks in the walls, and something resembling a gerbil sitting on his chest staring at him, apparently attempting to ascertain if he was still alive or not. The animal in question looked so agreeable, he would have rather not irritate it. On the other hand, he needed to eat. The glow in the room waivered as though the link that gave it control was experiencing difficulty keeping the association going.

Standing up took a few seconds because for some cause, while not mainly adverse to killing insects, these small cockroaches looked so delicate and shy he hated to diminish their population.

So, he held up until they'd found their different concealing spots before setting his feet down on the floor. This felt something like when Cassandra got her dope. One-more depressed spot in his life. Though not so much this time, since he'd had that to look back on.

He headed for the access and out into the storm toward the motel's main quarters for what he hoped would be something edible.

The after-hours was sharply cold, and the ice was descending in cans. Or was that lone downpour that did that? What did ice come down in?

He endeavored to consider anything shrewd but wouldn't. Not the manner in which he was competent.

When he resolved the principle building where the owner obviously lived, he entered the front entryway as he had before.

Not remembering the exact time, he had no idea what to expect. But whatever it was, he didn't expect what he found.

The man who he'd scarcely met and given his street-address only a couple of hours past, had not cooked supper. Nor was he pushing to fix any meals soon. At least not in this world. He lay face down on the counter with the back of his skull bashed in to the point that Francis could hardly recognize its shape. He didn't bother to test his pulse for any other signs of life.

Someone had accomplished a thorough job in ensuring he wasn't going to make him dinner. But who didn't originate after him. Curious. Whenever asking the owner would absolutely have given them his name. Why not? Unless there was a law against such things, and hc'd preferably offered his life over reprieving that law, were locals that stubborn? Assuredly most North Dakotans were not.

He scanned the place over for pieces of information the executioners may have left as to their names. Or whether they'd left anything to identify him as the culprit. Add another murder to his sheet of offenses. Unfortunately, he'd long overlooked what he'd touched when he conveyed and examined he hadn't been clever enough to fake his name. There would be that.

The murderers wouldn't need to worry about it. He'd left a lot of proof of his individual name and locale origin. Chicken soup had not been a very big lunch, and for a second he contemplated carrying the dead proprietor back to his pantry and make himself the dinner he'd been promised for his payment, though that appeared mainly heartless. He did relieve the man of his money. He never again would require it. And he should leave his fingerprints on the register too. Why not?

Francis realized he'd be accused of this homicide. No need to be subtle about it. Be that as it may, though, where to go? The storm had turned it up a notch, and a look out the door made it obvious he wasn't about to go far in the newly acquired inches of fresh snow piled up everywhere. It was additionally clear it wouldn't be a smart move to stay there with the dead body.

He switched off the lights.

Perchance a delay in the discovery for a while.

He closed the door prudently, and headed down the driveway for the main highway in hopes of finding some kind of shelter for the evening and the nourishment he now desperately needed.

If not to make the thundering in his stomach stop to keep his frame temperature over the point of solidification.

The road when he got there, was knee deep in newly fallen sleet. Zero traffic and no plow or salt trucks making their rounds. Visibility had fallen to about ten feet or so, even standing beneath a street lamp as he now was.

It was excellent and savage at the same time. Beautiful as the snow swirled and changed directions with the varying breeze. Deadly as he became aware that he couldn't survive very long out here. Unluckily, he wasn't beyond any doubt which heading to go given his failure to detect anything facing north.

He went left to keep his frame parts rousing, and on the grounds that he figured he could detect diminished lights out there. Whale of an evening. He looked back to seeing the motel manager dead in his bureau, concern that a couple of years ago conceivably he could have triggered him to feint or toss his cookies, but now was anything added than one added glitch in an otherwise terrible dream of resembling held glitches so commonplace it scarcely it merited a second thought. It annoyed him to be so heartless about it, yet authenticity can do that to you. For a while at least. He'd probably hate himself for it later on.

The shine he'd seen became gradually bigger and he understood he'd scared it rich.

Then he saw an evening coffee shop. Open. Lights completely on and a few customers in seats with their cars and trucks in the parking area covered with ice. They'd not be rushing anyplace soon. He could, at any rate, get a decent supper and perhaps, quite possibly, find a spot he could go through in the dark. Or heaps of espresso and he'd have no inconvenience not resting. He advanced there with some trouble and pulled the entryway open.

The breeze shut it trailing him, and he wound up in the little internal sanctum that such places have in virus atmospheres. A two-entryway framework to enable clients to get over the hail and enter the foundation spotless and invigorated. So, he did.

One of the two waitresses he could identify, showed him to a booth near an aperture and he asked her the question of the night. With a lie in there to boot. His car broke down a little way out of town. He wondered on the risk that he could take cover here for a period until they cleared the street. Hell, purchase the costliest supper in the house. Beyond any doubt. That's what every other person is planning. That's what he's doing. All anybody can do. And you don't need to purchase the costliest supper in the spot either, in spite of the fact that it wouldn't really cost that copious.

"They serve pretty cheap food here. All of it. Though by shoddy, I don't mean terrible. It's actually very good." And she kept on like that for as long as he could take it. As she talked, he picked up a menu and pointed to what he wanted. She talked as she recorded the request, and in the long run disregarded him. He wasn't beyond any hesitation about what to study about her. Probably on a caffeine downing spree. He settled back in the false calfskin plastic seat and pulled his jacket down about his midriff and rested.

Conceivably everything was turning upward.

Later he noticed that most of the other customers looked like truckers caught in a storm. Big heavy guys talking like they discerned each other. Comparing accounts of past snowstorms they'd persevered in, didn't see any cops about. They'd no doubt be tending a warm flame at central station as full hostages of the weather.

He walked over to a table and got a rebel paper left there by someone else's client trusting upon expectation he wouldn't discover his image on the primary page. He didn't come-across it there or anyplace else so far as that was concerned.

His snappy examination didn't uncover even a short section about the New York murder binge, or his alleged contribution. Relieved that his luck may have changed, he put his elbows on the table, the very same elbows he'd used earlier that day to disable one of the stooge-type characters who'd been following him, and let his head fall into the palms of his hands. He dreamed of sitting on the couch with Cassie beside him, watching the fire sparkle and pop in front of them and imbibing a glass of straight hooch with no one trying to capture, follow, maim, or shoot him. It was nice. He must have fallen napping then, for the waitress that wouldn't stop talking tapped him gently in order to serve him his steak and eggs over easy with a large pot of coffee on the side and a generous portion of lemon pie as well.

Possibly it wasn't Cassie by his side and a fireplace to sit in front of, but surprisingly life felt pretty good anyway. He surveyed the hail fall for some future through the window by him. The breeze had decisively stopped blowing, so challenging and the ever-different flakes drifted down into the icy dunes that lay beneath them.

No sky in sight.

At one point, he attempted to make sense of what had transpired to him and contemplate that fateful day when two men hit him outside his apartment in North Dakota.

But he recognized that except for a few threads, most were not tied together. Eventually he decided to study about what he did for a living beside think. Unreal life. Against Von Neumann's extraordinary concepts of machines begetting machines to John Conway's wonderfully simple software called game of life which many sites on the internet made popular.

Of Chris Langtons now renowned, yet then put able meetings at Los Alamos and retained at the Santa Fe Institute in New Mexico. Of John Holland's exceptional work with hereditary calculations and complex versatile frameworks. Of Karl Simms and his evolved creatures, now of all things a screen saver. What's extra of Aristad Lindenmayers l-frameworks, a basic calculation that produces models of plant development.

Every one of these scholars and researchers broadening the limits of both their meanings of life and nonetheless few trusted their ideas of making virtual lifeform innermost a computer. Aside taken quantum material science and cosmology, the most energizing field in present AI science sitting tight for original disclosures that appeared to happen each day.

He kept pouring down the coffee that the all-night talkathon waitress kept bringing him. Over the room he saw that huge integers of truckers had cogitated it a nightfall. Napping in their chairs as they probably had so habitually in their truck seats parked alongside a highway somewhere. He would have done likewise had it not been for the measure of caffeine he'd doused. In the long run, a second server clearly beat with the absence of anything besides wheezing and white stuff delicately falling outside the casement decided to join him.

CHAPTER 12.

The sunshine passed. The weather controlled and nothing occurred. Absolutely nothing. No blowing wind of merit and little to do but hike up the umbrella to shelter himself from sunburn, consume sleep, and generally bore himself senseless.

Actually, the highlights of his days, when not engaged in such mundane matters, he spent his opportunity thinking of previous adventures in his life. Mostly about his experiences with insane people, while endeavoring to do his examination of them.

That primary time he met Cassie, not that she was insane, but the situation in which she'd trapped him was that she had apparently died or at least he believed she had in his arms in the middle of a snow-covered meadow in North Dakota.

Then she'd died once again, clubbed to fatality on their primary date.

Afterward she'd been a psychiatrist.

And following that, a librarian.

All the while different individuals endeavored to kill him. What a ride. An outing to the Big Apple to spare the world by making a computer infection for which no one but he could provide the fix. Make billions by bilking computer users at ten bucks apiece. All to no end when the arrangement ended up living purely on analysis, or some likeness thereof, to trap fear mongers who didn't actually exist.

He was never exactly sure what he was doing between buying dope for a meth-head to living accused of multiple murders and wanted by every law enforcement agency in the world it appeared.

After that his wonderful encounter with semi-local American Indians and what he called the lifers because of their bent on killing him to save lives.

Plenty of violence there he could still feel. All ending with an insane woman blowing herself and part of him to kingdom come. And a previous slow-up of years episode in the rocky foothills of Canada where he used an analog computer to supposedly release electrical reproductions into the atmosphere to destroy some of the excess carbon-dioxide there hoping to reverse the effects of global warming.

And like all the earlier plans driven by a madman, who died at his brother's hand. What a ride. Add one ship down and living mislaid in the waters of a sea bedecked with icebergs, and it all made for an excitingly precarious and pointless series of adventures. Was he any closer to discovering his fantasies? Of creating life? Of discovering the wonders that made him what he was? Alive?

Or was he only wandering through a minefield waiting for the big one to get it over with? Was he in search of demise not reproduction? Every one of these contemplations and numerous others crossed his forlorn personality as the days passed. Not an indication of anything taking place after a scan for overcomers of the sunk freight transport.

Perhaps they assumed they'd rescued all the persons aboard the ship except the Captain and equally assumed he'd too gone down with his ship like all good Captains did. Or should. Whatever.

As he struggled with these memories and projections of his present condition, he contemplated his examination itself. Truly it got staggering exposure, yet so what? So do mass murderers. Yes, he got promoted and the money so attained made life easier to bear. But so what? He could have inherited the money. No difference.

Yes, his work was exciting. No one believed otherwise. Be that as it may, however, what had he actually created? And would he ever know when he'd attained it.

How did that information arrive? Maybe it would originate as it regularly did as terrible news. As an unbelievable infection or something unquestionably hurtful than great. Shunt them rapidly back to the Stone Age.

In this manner, was his examination happier falling flat than succeeding?

Without any end in sight.

No doubt about their intentions any longer. After him or them all the way. He grabbed the doorknob and tested it. Locked. He gave it a jerk forward and suddenly outward, unsure of which way it moved. No go. Likely secured against central.

He yelled, "Look out for Cassie," soon-after he stepped back and gave it a hell of a blast with his foot. Enough to break someone's leg. Hated to squander his vitality, yet what the heck. Their lone way out. It gave. Not the total entryway, just the wood in its within.

His foot broke through into open space beyond. Not enough room to crawl through, but a start. He punched out something sufficiently significant for one of them to get an opportunity to make it inside. This, just as the throng on the attack hauled ass toward them, now aware that they'd found a possible loophole in their plans. As soon as the hole was big enough to let Cassie through, he pushed her innermost. No opportunity to clarify.

Next, he changed to look at their pursuers. Still not enough glow to tell who they were or how many, but he didn't actually give a damn. He dropped to the pavement as the primary of them charged him, and then later he crawled between sets of legs as far as possible until it became clear the mass of humanity jammed in-between the two walls had figured out what he'd accomplished and where he had to be.

At that point, he got to his feet rapidly and, utilizing his elbows, knees, and head butts, endeavored to do as loads of harm as he could.

Bodies fell near him. A couple of passes up, then he was numbed. Just a vocation to do. No feeling.

He'd learned to rid himself of that enemy.

Let his regular medications do their work. Keep as sensible as could rationally be expected. The night, even of early-to-mid-dawn, and especially in the shadows of such high buildings, worked in his favor. While he was one and they were numerous, it was strangely to his advantage. No gamble of his hurting anyone on his side.

They again were doing as loads of harm to their very own as to him. In the end, he tripped into a mass of limp bodies at his feet and let them tear each other separated from him.

He did whatever it took not to move. Whenever a leg went by, he bit it as problematic as would be prudent and heard the subsequent cry. Occasionally he smashed a clenched hand upward into what he trusted was a crotch.

In return, he got thrust in the head, scared in the stomach, originated falling bodies, and stomped on. He misplaced his breath a couple of times and could feel his blood ooze from various wounds. Fair enough for what he was dolling out.

Was this what he'd learned originating fighting the bear. Concentration over matter? But did he have a decision to make? Notwithstanding thinking these thoughts, he found that checking shouts demonstrated fulfilling. Every part of one's form is a weapon. These guys didn't know that. They most likely played by some quality of standards yet weren't mindful of it. He had only one rule. Win. At any expense. Execute the lion.

Win.

Next someone decided to uneven the score. It looked like one of those phony pops that one hears in old western movies. Clear enough to him, however. Gunfire. One or more of them had decided to end it here and now, on the gamble that the concept cleared the back road.

At that point, he heard additional shots.

He'd asked that Cassie wouldn't holler. That she wouldn't give herself away. She didn't.

He kept biting and breaking bones with his arms and legs as he could. When anyone encompassing him endeavored to get up, he ensured they remained down. Hurting now, though he didn't give a damn.

Lastly the thing settled down. No extra slugs, just alarms. Somebody had called the cops. Also, his enemies.

He stood up and endeavored to walk. Stumbled. Couldn't tell whether it was an injury or several bodies on the cement below. Eventually he made it to the access hole in which he bent over and crawled inside.

That's when the lights went out. Someone hit him on the head with something hard and metallic. Like a frying pan. Who would have a skillet internal to their secondary passage. Didn't appear to consider who or what he'd finished studying, he was longing for a kinder and gentler spot where nobody was attempting to slaughter or debilitate him. Or take his thoughts. Was there such a spot? Most likely not on earth.

He longed for an ocean so certain that one could observe the base and all the fish swimming between him and that base. Like you detect in leaflets about Hawaii or the Bahamas. Snorkeling. The fish red and green, and the various unthinkable hues that fish just wouldn't be. Warm waters. Very little waves. Just enough to rock him back and forth like presence in his mother's arms when he was a baby.

At that point, he woke up.

CHAPTER 13.

Francis then contemplated calling Jackson, his foul-mouth colleague and friend at the university. He'd bailed him out of past scratches a few times before, and him he could trust. He'd even had his house ransacked, car blown to smithereens, and various other calamites rendered on him that made him a first-hand contributor to his self-preservation society. Of course, he'd also unwittingly contributed to the enemy's knowledge of him, but he divined that given his specialty was psychology. Arriving to consider he'd been more of a dolt than an advantage at times, Francis put him on the reserve list for now.

Cassie was his Achilles Heel, and while she'd absolutely volunteer to assist, she'd also hightail immediately to her brother Patton, the Chief of Police in their fair college town, someone who'd spent higher stakes trying to place him in jail for his own good than not. No.

And with that he realized that, as popular as he was with the press, he was also unpopular with many men and women in the university, faculty, and students. He was also sure that was because of his screwball—in their minds at least—takeoff from his personality.

But it still irked Francis that so many took the bait and supported him when most he needed it. As he entered the liquor store, the entryway tinkled a little ringer. One man behind the counter. No other customers. Couldn't be better. Things were at last turning in his direction.

He found the whiskey and set out toward the clerk. On his way there, he walked by a pile of newspapers and something grabbed his attention. He stopped and changed his course. The anything that had caught his eye was a piece on the front page of the Times titled *Serial Killer On The Loose*. Not something to be thankful for. However, an awful element for somebody resembling a bum with a great deal of cash in his pocket. Wandering throughout the city with no spot to remain.

He picked up the paper and read a few lines. Apparently, some nut had taken to murdering vagrants in the Queens area leaving bodies covered in heaps of junk.

Six such casualties to date. All tied to one person. A murderous crazy person name of Will Francis from the great state of North Dakota.

And a picture. One fortunately without whiskers. His driver's license photo when he had his wallet.

No further information of worth.

Presently he wasn't that fascinating a person. His mouth faltered open. Doesn't that always happen when you read a story like this about yourself? Bokator wouldn't assist him out of this jam.

He sat down in the aisle and imbibed some of the bottle of booze. Unfortunately, that wouldn't have seemed so great to the owner without his paying for it. Or the police, who'd positively track him down soon enough.

So, he breathed as softly as he could and once again headed to the counter as he had before to pay for his hellish sin. At that point, he understood what he may resemble to the person behind that counter. A killjoy utilizing a hundred-dollar note to purchase his preferred medication of decision.

But suddenly he figured this was New York City. Who gave a damn? Right? Right! He certainly didn't.

The clerk took Francis's bill and pushed it into his 1940s money register, made the transformation, and sent him out the entryway.

Francis peeked back to detect if he was making a phone call.

He wasn't.

So, he headed back through the street to the forest and park. He needed to sit a couple of minutes to peruse the story and get things straight in his mind before unwrapping his container of liquor.

He found a street light and a seat neighboring the walkway with some luminosity, and sufficiently concealed that he wouldn't be so noticeable against the road he sat next to, and read through the primary page piece. He had apparently, and within a single night's rampage, murdered many completely defenseless drunks providing a trail of self-identifying business cards and other identification originating from his mislaid wallet.

Obviously, a damn moronic activity.

He'd also apparently shot and wounded the Chief of Police in a small college town in North Dakota a week or so before identified by his fingerprints on the weapon used to shoot him.

Patton.

No motive given.

He was obviously a man gone out of his mind. Every cop in New York and North Dakota and parts between were BOLO. 'Be on the lookout.' Any suspicious character ought to promptly be grabbed and conveyed for a street-address.

He kicked back and gazed at the sky, as yet releasing delicate wet pieces of hail at him. He was one hell of a bad guy. Probably should be shot on sight. No inquiries posed.

He attempted to figure it out. Every concept started with the lights rushing out. Had that been a mishap or intentional? Could Cassandra (not Cassie) have been lying about the entire city pushing dark? Was her hundred-dollar blessing to him an endeavor to pay him back, or had she explained to him how to plant the cash to make it simpler for him to get away?

Was Masters involved?

He wouldn't have to shoot him, he'd let the police do it for him. Or his competitors. Whoever got to him first.

He thought of calling Cassie. Try to explain everything. Would she trust him? Patton was her brother. More importantly, was she still alive?

He had no idea any longer who to trust.

Who to go to.

Who would believe him.

He needed to run.

But where? And to what end? This for a computer infection with an antivirus not a long way behind.

As he sat in the half-light and let the snowflakes collect on his borrowed fur coat, he let his shoulders droop and his attention grow pitifully sullen. And further, it had once been so simple.

He shut his eyes for a second and took it all in profoundly. The self-indulgence wouldn't assist him at all.

What to do?

Initial order of business he had to get out of The City. He endeavored to imagine what encompassed it in his psyche. Long Island materialized strolling into an impasse. Sure he could get there, elementary enough, for Queens was on the south and slightly west side.

Except once out of the city, he'd have water on three sides and no spot to go.

If any of those after him found his area, it would be genuinely simple to chase him. North would take him along the coast aiming up towards New Haven. Yale. Probably safe there, though again water on one side and a town jam-packed with students on the other.

Be that as it may, superior to Jersey to the west and south. But Jersey took him closer to North Dakota. But wasn't that where he wanted to go? Patton was beloved. If the town saw Francis as his attempted murderer, he'd be in jail without a lawyer, especially as the sufferer was the brother of the town's public defender as well as his beloved Cassie.

Francis lay against the back of the seat, stared upward, and shut his eyes. Anything would have been loads simpler in the apartment he had in the Masters Building. Why'd he need to leave?

Perchance CM had been right. His followers had ordered him to never lie. The sleet descended earnestly and adhered to the asphalt before him. He tested the paper for the weather forecast. Heavy storm heading into The City. Half a foot expected. He peeked down.

Streets deserted.

Everyone home before their chimneys, hanging tight for the innovative layer of white to make their end of the week an eager one.

If, in actuality, it was an end of the week, he really had no idea, he had to get motivating. Remaining out in the exposed would likely—even with his facial hair and coat—transform him into an icicle a little while late.

"Yale," he said to nobody specifically.

North.

New Haven.

And he walked to the nearest subway access.

He pulled up his collar as anyone would do in this weather, hopefully making him less conspicuous. And less recognizable.

He found the closest real convergence and progressed strolling.

Had to be metro stairs adjacent. It took him just ten minutes to come-across an entrance course and go down the steps to pay for his ticket and load up a train.

Seeing a clock on the divider demonstrated one in the primary parts of the bright. Explained the absence of travelers. A great time for him to take the subway. Also, a decent opportunity to get robbed. In any case, though, he could deal with himself, so the anterior held didn't trouble him that much.

The train he picked went through Manhattan, crossed beneath a recreation center at that point, traveled north for the huge stations where he'd need to switch trains. Had to keep awake through this section so he kept his head buried in the Times like a late to get home bookkeeper.

It worked.

No one stood in his way or materialized to care about his presence at night in a mostly empty car in the New York City subway system.

After switching trains, he once again found himself buried in a newspaper caring not the least what the politicians said, or who had made so numerous billions in the stock market, or who had shot whom in a last-minute night bar fight. Only about him.

He'd have rather looked at the comics, though the adhered edition didn't seem to carry them. He figured he may have cried by then. Not a sobbing kind of crying, but a tearful sorry for himself kind of crying. Everything had gone his way so far but things were now getting worse. How could the boring existence of a university professor get so damn scrambled.

His father had once told him to cavort the hand dealt him. 'I'm trying, dad.' he thought, 'but the decks are stacked against me.'

On the other hand, he was warm, had some money in his pocket, and a bearing in which to travel. What could be better than that?

His mom had once guided him to never overlook a probability. Had he?

What in the event that he essentially convoluted and reappeared to in the Masters Building? Would they let him in?

Bygones be bygones.

Or what if he called Cassie and explained the situation. If she were home, hospital, prison, or a thousand other places he wished he could be with her.

Would she let him into her life again? Would Patton trust him when he recuperated. Could he turn himself in to the New York City police and explain what had actually happened?

Would they trust him?

His dad had been correct. Too many ifs on his mother's side of the equation.

He had to gamble it as dealt. He was wanted for several murders with plenty of evidence against him.

No inkling whether Masters was following him or not. Probably not.

Would he turn him in on the possibility that they'd discover him?

The competition, two of which he'd clobbered a while back near his apartment in North Dakota were probably lurking somewhere nearby, waiting for some kind of lead to corner him.

Suddenly what?

Someone else, an extra violent version of what Masters had forced him to do. Have to build up some other viral freak to convey a new debacle to the world.

He fell asleep thinking of all the possibilities.

He woke to someone tapping insistently on his shoulder.

Annoying.

He actually bounced to his feet readied to take on anybody within reach, yet all he found was a silver-haired older representative in uniform performing his responsibility.

"Sorry sir. End of the line. You'll need to get off here."

Regulations. He shook some of the cobwebs lose. He'd originated neighboring to unleashing a beast ready to kill the lion. He came to his senses.

Of course he expressed his gratefulness to him.

"Fell asleep. Sorry."

"No problem, sir."

He would have grabbed all his stuff soon after if he'd had any stuff to grab. Apparently, the newspaper he'd speedily read when he fell snoozing had gone to the nearest vagrant on board.

As he left the train, the sun scanned over the station rooftop in New Haven. One more fresh start for a serial killer. No place to go and a lot of future to arrive, he strolled up a squat slope and left some point neighboring what he accepted that was downtown.

The traffic was light at this early morning hour, so he crossed wrongfully apropos a little café that seemed open for breakfast. A satisfying little fly on a corner. A couple of bagels and three or four cups of coffee last-minute and he was fit as a fiddle. Whatever that meant.

In light of no goal with the exception of namelessness, wherever he went he walked on what the signs demonstrated were the grounds of Yale University.

He struggled to reminisce if he knew any faculty there. At least somebody who may be keen on AI and wouldn't know any concept about his last-minute shameful past. None rang a bell.

But there must be a library he could visit. Something to shield him from pondering his present situation. Perhaps gain some innovative useful knowledge.

With the assistance of two or three understudies, he found the library and obviously they enabled free rule of the stacks to anybody. Just couldn't take out any books without a library card.

He chose to dismiss any endeavor to discharge his mind of his present pickle, sat in the newspaper area, and read about himself. Notice, if he'd been up to anything new in the past few hours while he slept. Perhaps he'd murdered some further humans while he slept. Obviously, he'd become even more acclaimed over the earlier week or something like that.

Shouldn't locate a solitary newspaper without one story covering his adventures. And most had the same picture, no misgivings against his mislaid driver's license. Ridiculous photograph. So terrible that with his facial hair presently developed, he couldn't envision anybody remembering him. At least here in Yale country.

He envisioned that he looked academic here. Heavy jacket and a recognized mop of hair on his head. Who, possibly, could figure he'd carried out such disturbing wrongdoings? He'd accomplished just the same old elemental and original sins since the article he'd read in the Times. In fact, his apparent homicidal spree had stumped the authorities. For as hastily as he'd committed the killing of humans, he'd mysteriously halted. Ran away without a trace. Even a national manhunt had claimed no hints of his whereabouts.

Surprisingly, given everything that had ensued on his little adventure, this made him blissful. Enough, at least, to seriously examine calling Cassie. She'd believe him. Wouldn't she?

He repeated his need for a phone to the main desk and asked to make a long-distance call. The librarian glanced surreptitiously and handed him a phone from under the counter.

CHAPTER 14.

Around seven in the after-hours with Jackson as of yet prowling about, he chose to set out homeward bound in the night. He needed to prepare for his Monday classes and get some rest.

Francis, dressed in his sundry coats and boots headed across the meadow separating the Computer Science Building and his apartment. Thank God Jackson didn't tail him in spite of the fact that he was starting to comprehend his interest about him and his lab. Jackson also had a lab, but nothing in it would keep understudies working there twenty-four-seven. Against the lab directors' instructions, yet.

They may have gotten themselves into a mess, but it was an exciting mess. As he approached his condo, somethings stood out.

First, his lights were on. He hadn't left them that way.

Second, Cassie's car was parked on the street out front. He understood he hadn't given her directions to his place, but their advanced jail flare-ups had initiated them full of concern.

They did generally speak at least once a day. Satisfied his after-hours may be spiced up a little, he opened his façade entryway with added eagerness than he ordinarily would.

Unfortunately, that vanished the moment he ventured innermost. Sitting on his sofa was the largest person he'd at any point seen in his life. A giant. Possibly seven feet tall, but obviously not a basketball player, for this guy was huge in every way. Not fat by any means, mostly muscle bulging beneath the suit he wore. Dusky whiskers and scarring around the eyes. Definitely not Cassie. He could tell that right off.

He peered at him staring at him.

He shut the access door wondering if he should have shut himself out rather than in. But, as they say, the bigger they are the harder they fall. For his situation, he could end it with a clenched hand to the crotch. Right at his eye level. Of course, he scanned like conceivably he had metal balls. Maybe they could do more harm to

Francis than the giant. A true eight-hundred-pound gorilla.

When he arrived in the AI area at the U, and landed in his office chair, it was the exact opposite he recalled until he woke to the smell of espresso preparing.

The giant was sitting in his agency chair. Warm, nonetheless wet. He had apparently had a nightmare he'd disregarded that made him sweat a lot.

Francis's coats, which he could have sworn he'd left downstairs, were hung neatly within his workplace door. They also seemed wet. Or at the least moist. Perhaps someone had borrowed them for a tour of the sleet outside. Whatever.

He headed out the door, forgetting for a second he was in his agency and not home in his bedroom.

He abruptly ceased and stuffed his shirt into his jeans and attempted to brush his hair with his fingers. He found the espresso preparing in the parlor and grabbed a couple of containers.

Not bad for instant. Except not coffee. Caffeine at least.

His gathering was in the lab. Jackson had evidently dozed in or chosen he'd attempt to overcome the atmosphere outside. Or perhaps he was stowing away in the men's room hesitant to confront him after their ongoing verbal debates.

The big guy sat in the corner drinking coffee and not enjoying it much. He seemed depleted. He rebounded to his office and rapidly got dressed, adding two coats to his completed wardrobe. He then walked back to the lab and as quietly as conceivable tiptoed into his area of research.

Then, he waited to check whether anybody heard him. Silence. The arrangement was straightforward. Jerk the door exposed unpredictably and hightail outside into the dark and down the street apropos the Police Department only a few blocks away.

He shouldn't imagine anyone expecting this tactic. Primarily they'd assume he was still sleeping, and second if not napping, he hadn't seen the cop, and third, if he was wrong about the primary two assumptions, they'd guess he'd try to block the entrance.

Never expect him to charge out the access and into the night. Bokators don't run from fights. Chess games maybe, but not Bokators. He readied himself by mentally checking the outside entrance to make sure he didn't run into a wall or a garbage can.

Of everything else blocking his way, this was the point at which he heard it. Soft thumps on his entryway next to him as though somebody definitely comprehended he was in his office.

He stopped.

Again the knocks.

If he'd been five feet further away, he'd have never heard them.

What to do?

See who was there?

Hold up until he butted it in?

Lock it again quickly?

He'd placed him precisely in the place he would have liked to place him.

He eventually decided to expose the entryway. What the hell. So, he did. And there he stood. A mile tall and wider than a Buick. He filled the space so completely he couldn't detect anything past him.

It took some time for him to get her left shoulder high enough for him to pull the cloth under it and tie it with his one good hand. But he was successful and surveyed the blood pressure as he did. One down.

He had no idea how he'd tackle the other problem. Not just that it was bigger and in gentler substance, yet the fabric would not or couldn't at all make it all encompassing her whole physique with the end goal for him to tie it.

What had he been examining? As he sat back and glanced at each element over again, he recognized he shouldn't put anything into the wound for fear of serious infection, which perhaps could wind up more harmful than the wound itself.

What to do?

He needed a med kit. Had to be one around though no way could he make it down the ladder. Coming up had taken everything he had.

The sky lit brighter than the sun had made it, and rapidly following that the sound of a huge flare-up rocked his balance and down and onto his left side. He peeked up to unearth a huge mushroom cloud next to them. Not a nuclear flare-up, but a new parochial boat having after a fashion gone ballistic. Whether by suicide or by one of his slugs at last having its way with the diesel fuel he'd probably never know. Didn't matter. They were one step closer to safe harbor and that's what counted now.

As a sign of added luck, he saw the blood flowing from Cassandra's stomach wound had diminished. And stopped. On its own. Anything he hadn't relied on yet, a surprising piece of elegance.

He got to his feet, hobbled to the pilot's chair, and sat, all the while looking over the plethora of dials, knobs, switches, and so on, not unlike those on the cargo ship he'd managed to survive though far less in number.

Before she'd been hit, Cassandra definitely had placed their vessel on a course that, as indicated by the bearing, would lead them straightforwardly to Boston Harbor.

Impeccable.

No requirement for him to control medical aid to their place or bearing. Rolling at high speed and with the wind against his mask by the windshields both in vanguard of and over his head, life, at least for the second, seemed relatively safe and collectively in high gear.

We were moving home. At last. In any event, to the extent home was spoken to by the arena of the Red Sox's Green Monster.

As he watched the slow afternoon brilliance cast ever lengthening shadows of the boat on the water, he believed this woman who lay at his feet. Who was she, he didn't know? A companion. Apparently so. She'd either spared his life or acted the hero on a few events. But she'd also lied to him profusely. And he had no clue what she actually did with her life. Brilliant. No question about it. Prurient. Absolutely. But who did she work for, and could or would he ever believe her?

He thought of Cassie. What he'd put her through in the course of recent years. How had she put up with it? Was this what pulled her to him. Francis's insane life? Or was he rolling to settle down once married to her? So, some questions. What's a higher possibility, no answers.

He noticed back at the dashboard and saw his foretell opportunity of entry. Two hours left. Slightly after dark. Would he have the option to discover the vessel into dock or would the autopilot do that for him? One could only hope it would.

Noticing the temperature had dropped several degrees in the anterior late half hour, he viewed the mist dotting the skies to the west. Another storm on its way?

He checked the dashboard again, though he couldn't come-across anything marked fittingly that revealed to him any anything helpful. And the mists could be obscuring taking the divine sunset as direction instead of a jam packed out tempest. At least one could hope.

He listened to the engine whine. A reassuring sound in these unreassuringly times. René was gone. And now likely the Kid. That left Leslie and him from the team, with her out of it according to Cassandra. The likely suspects next in this deviant plot had diminished. Or conceivably they hadn't.

Conceivably, the plot next for the coast guards endeavor to murder him was a different arrangement. Triggered by somebody he didn't know or in any event somebody he didn't suspect.

Furthermore, who were those suspects? Perhaps Leslie was faking it. Or René not dead. Had the Captain really gone down with the ship? Or next again, had the CIA fellow who apparently had terminal malignant growths really passed on? Was he somewhere alive?

And what about Boris Carlov? Hadn't heard about him for quite a while. Consider that he considered if there were as yet numerous applicants accessible, regardless of whether the probability of the vast majority of them certainly being alive or sufficiently perilous to do this minute.

As he stayed there tuning into the engine and gazing at the ocean, he napped once more. Continually worn out, openly originating his experience in the North Atlantic.

When he woke with his back harmed from twisting about and laying his look on the vessel's dashboard, it was dim and before him lay the lights of what he assumed was Massachusetts Bay.

Welcoming and anticipating him into its well-proportioned chest. Cape Cod to the south and Boston dead center—though his choice of words less than welcoming await—and Gloucester to the north as he remembered it taken his postgraduate daylight at MIT, though this future not originating from the same perspective.

The autopilot had accomplished its mission. At least the dials conveyed their way as heading directly inward facing the Boston Harbor shipyard and marina. Like following a prescribed beacon for their return.

The atmospheric pressure had actually twisted colder and he saw no stars above. He saw Cassandra resting. Still doing well. He ventured to the pilot's seat and checked her heartbeat. Strong, except she was shuddering against the cold. Bending over her and with a gentleness he didn't know he had, he laid her on her back as cautiously and lightly as he could. With so much weight lost from his diet of kelp extra kelp and even further kelp, he didn't evaluate his physique weight would fabricate any further loss of blood and conceivably could keep her warmer than direct exposure to the night air. And the wind which he now noticed had picked up, had taken over the west.

So, he covered her as best as he could, and soon the only two on board were sleeping together and keeping one another as warm as possible this night.

CHAPTER 15.

As he drove west from town, Francis attempted to reminisce about what he'd discerned about where he was going. A thousand or so square miles of land decreased in size essentially by a store on the Missouri waterway. Lake Sakakawea they called it. The whole Indian reservation was involved by encompassing six thousand citizens.

New Town was situated in the northwest area of the rez, his real goal.

Three affiliated tribes and Francis had no clue which one his cousin belonged to. Feasibly, his cousin Walt Tallpine didn't either.

On any occasion, the locals were doing great with oil under the terrain and a betting club on top of it.

The moonless nightfall kept him focused on the broken white line in front of him, and the lack of traffic kept him fairly sure he hadn't been followed.

Of course, for all he discerned they had everything planted in his car to keep tabs on him. Perhaps the cops. Possibly the 'lifers,' the name for those that wished him to stop his artificial life research. Probably the former, for he was currently lawfully a part of one of the three groups on the rez.

When he eventually turned south and recognized he was almost there, the magnitude of what they'd scheduled shocked him. Somewhere he'd never been before. Visiting a relative he hadn't seen in decades. One he'd not coexisted with in any case. On his turf. Not one-more part of the state, but a world apart.

Now a cop no less. Without a firearm since he hadn't been given one. Didn't ask, since he figured the answer would have been no.

Still missing, Cassie because Cassie was still missing. Heck of a thing. He'd been away for an hour and right now pining to returning home. What a trouper.

He passed the border marked only by a sign telling all who visited he was now entering the Fort Berthold Indian Reservation. Someone had taken a nail and X'd out the 'reservation' part, and scratched underneath it 'Nation.' As in the 'Fort Berthold Indian Nation.'

Already he felt like a foreigner.

New Town, however, peered like a twentieth-century village anywhere in the country. Possibly somewhat further decorated with cliché Indian axes, feathered hats, and bows and arrows from films, and so forth, yet generally the same.

He didn't know whether it made him copious, on edge about gathering with his cousin, or by and by in the nation searching for a location. Indeed, even in obscurity, he could tell the streets went level and straight. Elementary to pursue.

He arrived speedier than he needed to.

Still early.

And less than two hours from his apartment.

He, in the long race, pulled up before a one-story adobe house surrounded by grass and a soil garage. The house had luminosity on in the front window, and a vehicle left beneath a garage appended to the house.

In his headlights, Francis could detect the usual lawnmowers, snow plows, and various tools. Like the vehicle he drove, the one in the parking space had two lights on top for conveying the liable to equity.

It was later that he understood he wasn't actually a full-scale cop, not notwithstanding, for what he trusted would be a brief timeframe.

Leaving behind the other vehicle, he killed the motor and lights and took an occupied breath. Parking in front of the other car, he changed the engine and lights, and took a cavernous breath.

Everything was different about visiting a relative than visiting someone you don't know. Uncomfortable. At least for him.

He sauntered up the façade stairs and rapped on the entryway and paused.

No response.

He knocked once again.

This opportunity added intense and for other drawn out time. Then he heard a sound originating from inside. His gut agitated a bit as the covered window next to the front door opened slightly.

He saw practically as he recalled that he wouldn't have recognized him had they'd seen one another while passing on a sidewalk. Possibly he hadn't heard him.

He knocked again. This time louder and for a longer time.

Then he heard a sound originating from within. His gut churned a little more. The entryway opened. He immediately remembered him, though he wouldn't have recognized him in ordinary circumstances.

He had books. Lots of them. All pertaining to the rights and privileges of American Indians as well as cultural histories of Native Americans and what the government owed them in promises never kept.

He had no uncertainty it was all valid somehow, nonetheless the odds of trading in for cold challenging currency was practically nothing.

If Walt had heard of Cassie's disappearance, he surely didn't show it. Then again, Walt was in his pajamas and Francis had obviously woken him up. Time for apologies, explanations, and bringing out a cot upon which Francis would sleep the night.

In the morning, Walt was gone and Francis on his own. He opted to take a drive. Get outside while the daylight was still generally youthful. Clouds had begun to frame in the west, and it resembled the pre-fall long before reaching an end. Indian summer some called it, yet he questioned numerous here did.

Walt had raided his pants for his keys and left them in Francis's borrowed cop car. An invitation for someone to steal it. Window exposed and everything. He shouldn't imagine anything so naïve on the reservation as to make crime that rare. But who knew?

Obviously, there was some type of composed or unwritten code on stealing squad cars on the rez. Considering New Town was on the northern brink of the reservation, he drove south to get a general view of things.

With the sun shining, he got a very different version of the landscape than he'd had at night. For the most part prairie as he had forecasted, yet the dynamic slopes astonished him. They gently led the road up and over in ways both predictable and surprising. Predictable, as in everyone uncovered an extra past. Surprising, in glow of the fact that several had little streams and trees at the base while others had a style of vegetation the slopes had.

The grasses held a kind of dusky luminosity and diminutive look, no uncertainty because of the heavy snowfall. They covered the sand like a carpet beckoning him to stop and roll over on them. He had attempted it once when he was youthful and stalled out by the fragile demons and placed in his bedstead with a few diseases as a result of it.

The street took him on a wonderful drive until he resolved an impasse at the waterway. Or an area of the lake. Whatever. Practically a mile crosswise over now, without any vessels in recognition or extensions he altered over seeing as the roadway entered the water as though it had once proceeded or it was a decent year for precipitation. He sensed it like the water had swallowed up the land and its level depended not on the dam so much as the number of storms that had passed. That is the point at which he understood he'd likely gone twenty miles and not seen one house or passed one other vehicle.

The need for electricity downstream, outweighed what the dam had accomplished for the reservation lands.

Feasibly. he could now understand a little better his cousin's bitterness.

Eventually he found New Town and investigated. He recollected that if there were twenty-four-hour markets, corner stores, cafés, just as a few upscale stores one would discover anyplace in America. In between these were businesses serving visitors with parochial novelties and trinkets supposedly made by Indians. On lifting one up and inspecting it, Francis found it had been made in China. It required a long opportunity to return to his home so far away from home.

As he drew closer to Walt's spot, he saw he still wasn't back. Apparently extended periods of hours for the nearby police.

But his little trip had relaxed him. A slice of Americana for the rare sightseer. In any case, his little trek had loosened him up. He went within and took a nap. After that he chose a book or two against the bookshelf and read for a period. He shouldn't have. Either these books were obscenely paranoid or America had been criminally negligent in dealing with those whose lands it had once stolen.

As he read it in the white afternoon light, the letters squirmed like snakes. While he recognized he was getting just one side of the story and probably a one-sided one if yet a fifth of what he read was genuine. It emerged that his cousin had correctly assumed all of the conjectures were likely correct. At least they placed the blame where it definitely belonged. Unfortunately.

Not taking care of business aside against holding feelings of resentment, wasn't going to transform anything. Walt materialized about six looking grizzled and beaten. Having no inkling what police work on the reservation held for him, Francis offered Walt a drink of alcohol taken from one of the bottles he'd brought along.

CHAPTER 16.

Each hour he approached or left the Computer Science Building on the grounds, he'd reflect back to the numerous undertakings that had plagued him there.

When he attempted to spare the life of a young lady who allegedly had been shot in the back. When he'd battled some bad guys encompassing there, and sometimes won. People have stood or climbed trees to shoot guns, explode bombs, or secretly watch him along here. A significant history for perhaps a quarter mile of knoll, a road intersection, and twenty or so yards to his condo right across the road.

All recollections.

Better that than actually experiencing them again.

To brighten the last-minute afternoon sky which was blue in concept, but a few cirrus clouds whisking their way eastward without a hint a storm was on its way. A wonderful method to end a cool, however not cold, fall day in upper central North Dakota.

As he walked, Francis thought of these things. And further of Cassie whom he'd not seen in months, and their up and coming marriage. She wanted a big reception. A once in a lifetime future costumed extravaganza that shouldn't have left him less interested in showing up.

He'd not informed her, of course, after all, how could he? Of course, she always wanted to know what he thought. Something worth being thankful for. Probably didn't matter. Regardless he'd have a mind pursuer alongside him for a mind-blowing remark. Or at any rate, for whatever length of time she could remain with him.

As he ventured to the cement curb—into a crosswalk no less—he heard a vehicle drawing nearer from the north. He looked and saw a dull Ford that would have boggled any weak-minded person approaching him at a moderate speed.

Probably above the limit, though not familiar for students on their way to or from class. He kept walking. As he did, he heard the driver put on the brakes and pull over to the side of the road. When he noticed, he and his nondescript Ford were parked longwise against the curb about thirty feet away. Across from the complex where he lived which had numerous condos leased by understudies.

So, he kept strolling despite the fact that the elements currently troubled him. Like a little tickle subsequently his ear.

Something, even everything wasn't quite right.

The inclination developed as the driver revved his motor a couple of times. Not a predominantly logical thing to do except not really threatening either. Weird. Like an understudy might do to awe his better half.

He kept going.

Next, with a precipitous squeal of tires, the student or whomever floored the Ford and headed directly for him. Not logical. The engine had openly been souped-up or traded with someone else all the new dominant one for the old vehicle rushed directly at Francis, emulating one of those enormous things in the diminutive races he'd seen on TV.

Smoke rose from the pavement and the engine shrieked for air and gas while two eyes peered through the half-light created by the slowly setting sun. No amount of Bokator, his Cambodian martial art of choice, had prepared him for this.

'Never escape,' the Master had said.

But he couldn't have meant this for cars attacking humans. Fortunate for him, every one of these problems ran through his head in a brief instant, even as his legs ran what his DNA had trained them to manage with no cognizant idea.

There was no uncertainty about the aim.

As he ran, the vehicle actually pursued his bearing and made a beeline for where he was moving, not where he was right now. Smart driver. Obviously well-schooled in the art of picking pedestrians off when in activity.

That was the point at which his Bokator kicked in easily. Knowing the vehicle's driver was envisioning where he would be in a specific count of seconds, he altered his pose into straightforwardly facing it without breaking stride, trusting the driver would be found napping and basically drive on by.

No sham.

With a flick of his wrist the Ford turned on him. Anything and everything his preparation had not anticipated.

A second to go. Relaxed as he probably could be, his legs leapt into the air as high as he could, tucked his legs in as neighboring to his physique as conceivable, and let what was going to happen, happen. And it did.

His adrenaline-fueled high jump now placed him well above the Ford's hood and its ornament, and below his now curled legs and the top of the car itself.

When gravity had its direction, he tripped on a harder surface than the vehicle—the road—and lay there.

He twisted his head quickly, and viewed the driver speeding into the distance, wondering how in hell he'd missed him.

He wasn't alone. For he, no uncertainty, pondered about that higher than him. It had not been his expectation to do this following his senses. The fact that it worked was incredible. Incredible with the exception of the reality he'd arrived on anything regrettable than the hood or top of the speeding vehicle.

He'd fallen on solid cement. The kind of surface roads in North Dakota needed to have to withstand the snow plow traveling them sometimes during the long winter months.

So, before he adulated himself, he checked his body parts for broken bones, separated supply routes and drained scraped spots. This wasn't precisely difficult to do, for the way he'd laid, virtually all of him was visible.

In the meantime, the wearing-off adrenaline never again masked the torment achieving his cerebrum, originating a few headings without a moment's delay, and he hurt all over. But he was living, and for the second at least that was the most important concern.

Whether he'd keep on living needed to arrive just short of the win.

Someone then came charging into the street to identify how badly he was injured. At least he presumed this was her motive.

She bent and pointed something at him. It was not unlike a gun.

Had they foreseen what he possibly could do, and placed a backup nearby to make sure they succeeded in fulfilling their plan. For good.

He then understood what she clutched.

Not a gun. A microphone. A small one attached to a cell phone, though apparently a microphone nonetheless.

Great God, had this all been a trick?

CHAPTER 17.

After several days, Francis was released from the hospital. Him and a sack brimming with prescriptions, ointments, and exercise diagrams. Oh, what fun.

Jackson drove him crosswise across town to his condo, and chose without his agreement, to live with him for a week. To tell him about his classes, he said, though Francis realized he only wanted to keep an eye on him.

Had Cassie been found she would have begun making arrangements for their wedding. Apparently, however, she trusted him and never said a word about it to him. Oh, and the little beasties did return home. They didn't kill their code. Only jailed them until they could determine what had actually happened. Life or not life.

It would turn out hesitant, no uncertainty, nonetheless he had his very own doubts about a definitive decision.

Sometime during his recuperation Jackson commented on the possible success or failure of their attempt at creating nascent life. As he now reminisced about it, Francis ordered him to forget his definition of life which he felt was too broad.

While he'd been gallivanting encompassing North Dakota and Montana, Francis had been reading and thinking about it.

"Choice," he said, "is not programmable. In its spot, he recommended five ideas that all the further precisely depicted lifeform as he got it. The major letters of these ideas shaped the abbreviation *scree*, a pleasantly framed word in its very own correctness which guaranteed he recalled what he let him know. He said it represented the concept 'self.'

Broad, he noted, but nonetheless a word with a clear meaning. The letter S stood for 'self,' or course. The letter C showed code meaning every self-included code; a copious portrayal of DNA, an internal recollection of survival systems. R obviously meant 'reproduce.' The first E represented evolve, and the second E 'environment.'

In straightforward terms, life to him meant *s*elves containing *c*ode as *r*eproduced, *e*volved in order to cope with an ever-changing *e*nvironment. And he added the word *scree* itself which meant a collection of small rocks at the base of an incline. A great continuous forever.

He was not sure he had the exact wording right, but the acronym remained etched in his mind.

They discussed his musings as future amid his recuperation. Possibly his enthusiasm therefore for his lab was newer than passing. So, he wasn't dumb after all. Regardless it allowed him a risk to study an option that was other than himself as his injuries mended, and for that he was thankful.

Cassie was obviously the biggest confusion in his life. Watching out for him or stirring the trouble pot. Who knew? Exactly not him. But where she was, nobody knew; especially not him.

He also discovered from Jackson that the puking, pooping, and peeing puppy that had raided his personal computer screen had left during his absence. Neighboring a resembling time, they detained their unaccounted-for beasties. Connected? He questioned it. Undoubtedly, the canine was one-more of the tricks pulled on him when he'd still been an individual apparently attempting to destroy religion. For at least a couple of months thereafter, he continuously thought of Cassie. Challenging to get someone like her out of his mind. So extraordinary. So messed up. He spoke to Walt infrequently these days, though he had no inkling what went incorrect with his sister.

Before long, nonetheless, she found a spot in his old history and he repeated to educating and his work in the lab.

As exceptional as his opportunity had been on the rez and in Montana, and how his point of view had changed with respect to his work, he recaptured at any rate a similarity to the importance his examination had for the world. Someone else's pieces of him regardless still ached for the possibility that genuine instead of fake reproduction was what made the difference. This made him examine Little John. Why he had overlooked his experience of about having butted the bucket in the sleet that after-hours and him sparing him. Possibly his skillful stupidity, even though he'd gone to save his life in the primary spot.

Perhaps he'd been stunned against almost solidifying or suffocating himself in the profound hail. Perhaps it was on the grounds that he'd understood the person was greater, and preferred extra brilliance over him, and notwithstanding his typical convictions he could have completed an added exhaustive activity. More than heat getting life.

Possibly it was because he now owed him one and he didn't want to, especially after he misplaced his life, while trying to save hers. Or on the other hand, it was conceivable there were a few hundred different reasons.

Additional opportunities passed.

New daytimes and other evenings. Strung together like a string of beads encompassing someone's neck. Anything to separate one from another. Doze and wake and feed and fish for further weed. All there was to it.

But the nights grew colder. And the wondrous ice sheets materialized to gradually develop once higher.

The Gulf Stream had begun its inevitable return home, to where it legitimately had an area. Still additional time passed and he gradually misplaced it. Whether against the hallucinatory dope he was ingesting, or only the loneliness of the long-distance boater. No idea.

If he survived his visits to a rehab center, a good psychiatrist would have to deal with his new habit. Otherwise he'd not be respectable to anyone.

Conceivably Jackson, his psychologist colleague back at their university in North Dakota, so far away now, would have some ideas.

Francis also believed in his wife-to-be Cassie often. What was she doing right now? Was she thinking of him just as he her? Or was he just a quick blurring remembrance?

What's higher than her sibling Patton? Would he wonder if his sister had settled on a decent decision in Francis? What's extra, his lab at the college. What conceivable inconvenience had his alumni understudies gotten themselves into during this time. Would he ever identify any of them again?

But mostly he languished and hallucinated.

What's added the day and evenings go as small mice might under the frontispiece of obscurity amid the dark.

CHAPTER 18.

Marching orders.

He hadn't briefed him on this. He wasn't organized in the least, and had nothing to say. He had no suspicion of how large the loads of these individuals really had as of now. Why him and not him?

They walked toward the façade of the huge room, seating a lot beyond them and plunked down. All aside against him obviously.

With no whiteboard, no projection possibilities, and no everything, he stood back of the podium and rearranged his thoughts. Such as they were.

Unfortunately, nothing came to attention at that second, given he'd had no knowledge about his presenting circumstances.

With no presentation beside from what Bill had said, and no hardware or paper on which to take notes, he hacked apprehensively and attempted to make sense of a start and opened his mouth. That familiar process worked. After a second or two, and Francis had spoken two words, the alarm went off again.

Damn.

The thing was uproarious. Everyone immediately covered their ears except for Bill. He jumped up and ran for the door. He immediately figured everything had gone wrong this time. Two alarms in the same day.

They again had no point in running.

So, they stopped their ears as well as can be expected, and took a peek at each other as though it would aid somehow or once more.

Cassandra (not Cassie), had she been there, would have strangely smiled as she looked at him. He realized what it likely meant, but hoped for anything less problematic.

One thing he believed about himself, if push came to push and she and he wound up in bed together, he'd lose the genuine romance of his relationship. Not that Cassie was a prude, but he would in all probability uncover his carelessness. Or in any event, feel remorseful each opportunity he had neighboring to her.

Townsend currently appeared confounded and somewhat startled. As if his clean world had come unhinged. Not used to this kind of treatment.

Cassandra was the most unreadable of them all. She looked as if she'd foretold this to happen.

As on the gamble that she was used to the direst outcome imaginable, and managed it constantly.

Stu was Stu or just stew. He'd keep running in circles, though at this point sat back in his seat, stood up on his legs, and gazed at his shoes. As if by one way or addition, the appropriate response lay in the tying of his hands there.

What an odd crowd of misfits. Both intense and ridiculous as his lab team at home.

The activity of the former halted, and the five of them breathed out all the while. He didn't know what to expect from them. No surprise if the militia came chasing into the room and drive them out like cattle.

Conceivably Bill could foretell backward to disclose the nearest to them that it had all been a mix-up. Or conceivably, the initial alarm, as loud as it was, had given their position away to whomever they were and they'd stormed the Bastille.

Before any of them got an opportunity to appreciate a concise snapshot of harmony, the sound impacted their eardrums once again. For the third opportunity that daytime. Feasible, the third occasions had an appeal he assumed that by and by hammered his index fingers into his ears to abstain his hearing.

He couldn't envision this was a sunshine to sunshine event. No one could continue working under these conditions. Either the state army's uniform accompanied programmed earplugs, or they'd by one way or another dealt with the madness of unforeseen earsplitting shrieks in their lives.

The sound stopped again. No journey so moronic

None of them unplugged their fingers this time. They peeked at one someone else again, and waited for the inevitable. Which of course never came. Rather, following a few minutes of soundlessness, Bill reemerged into the room grinning as he strolled. As he spoke, he clicked some quality of remote control in his grasp and the whole divider, conceivably sixty by forty feet, lit up with the yield named Blackie.

So dazed by the abrupt nebulous vision, he let out a whoosh of air. This he had not foreseen. There before them, in coloration and what must have been an astronomical figure of pixels, was the Lorenz attractor, the one come across by a weatherman of the same name some decades ago. An all-out picture of why mankind would never have the option to make precise weather forecasts past a specific numerical point.

The longer Francis looked at the image, the higher the detail emerged. This was not size for the sake of size, but size for visualizing complexity at unheard of scales. There was no doubt they were in the organization of the most elevated amount simple computer at any point constructed.

As they stared at the image, Bill adhered up his right arm and using his right thumb began changing one variable with a large knob on Blackie. The picture shook somewhat, became fluffy, and lastly vanished by and large in a labyrinth of complex visual clamber.

He got the picture.

"This is the largest screen of its kind in the world. Not for presenting films, but for real-time output from the world's largest analog computer."

He may have been bragging, yet the show was justified despite all the trouble. Whoever had figured this out had done an incredible job. Francis couldn't envision anybody other than him equipped for bringing it off. And indeed, he ended up changing his assessment of himself to one new significantly larger amount.

Townsend suggested a conversation starter which had at primarily irritated him too.

"This must be a digital image. Why were they taking a glance at an advanced picture, when what we're doing here is commending the God-like continuous possibilities."

He didn't need to put it precisely that way.

CHAPTER 19.

He sat in his room that night, both happy and disheartened. To comparative degrees.

He held in the wake of demonstrating the outlandish should be possible. Dejected because he was stuck in this giant coffin in the wilds of the Rocky Mountains in a winter storm with no way to escape and nowhere to go even if he could.

What a wreck.

Was Cassie missing him as endlessly as he did her, wherever she was at the moment? Was she practically finished with the wedding plans with thousands in attendance and him only a disordered groom? Was Patton mindful of his due date and them two currently pondering what had turned out badly? Had Jackson taught his classes? Was it summer vacation there with all his students gone to wherever they went during summers? He'd gotten so associated with his work, none of these contemplations had jumped out at him as of recently. Or they'd scared him to far less a degree than they ought to have. What a wreck.

Surprisingly, he heard a sound. Anything interesting regardless of a brush of delicate fabric against something hard. Familiar in this spot.

Their rooms had been adhered, taken each other, and hearing any reverberations with the exception of those he made himself was surprising. Someone else's sound.

He'd left his entryway exposed as he often did to give his space a slightly larger feel to it.

He stood quietly and walked to the already ajar access and peeked out into the hallway. There, remaining with his luck charged dry alongside his open entryway, was an occupied formally dressed workplace loaded with his rifle indicating the preparation for action.

Peculiar. Had never taken place before this. At least he believed not. He hadn't really viewed it before now, and perhaps just seen this future as a result of the noises he'd heard.

"Help you?"

No reaction. Like a watchman at Buckingham Palace, his straight-ahead gaze as sure and devoted as he could envision.

He sensed it like giving him a gentle shove on the shoulder to observe if he could to get him to respond, but he noticed the insignia on his uniform jacket arm. Not one of theirs. Or suddenly again, one of England's finest if mind served. Or one of any number of other countries whose insignia he would recognize.

What the hell was going on here?

He took a bursting breath and let it out gradually. Unwinding. Too much had occurred that day. Perhaps he was hallucinating. Or in any event, making a hasty judgment before he had enough actualities.

What did he know about the Green Berets, for example? Would they use patches such as the one he was looking at now? Lots of special forces out there in the military who could utilize such things. This symbol had a blade with circles of red and green encompassing it. Not the pigmentation he would think America would use. Those would incorporate red, white, and blue, wouldn't they?

His knowledge of the militia was he now realized slight at best. This, his initial sunshine on obligation here.

Knowing he wouldn't locate a solution, he didn't. Not by any means a conspicuous flicker of his eyes. He alleged about what he'd do, whether he chose to go to supper. Would he stop him? Follow him? Was he beneath house arrest? Or, on the other hand, was he here to monitor him?

Realizing his list of questions about what he was doing here had multiplied in the last minute, he gathered his wits and decided to get some answers. He sauntered out of his room, departing the exposed entryway, and took a right turn directly before his guest and said, "Dinnertime," trusting him in any event for the impression he was not endeavoring to escape, just reporting his aims.

At first, he didn't move. At least as far as Francis could hear and acknowledge he was hiking away from him. It was challenging to detect his facial and other physical indicators. So, he turned, and there he was. Tailing him as unobtrusively as would he be prudent.

Still at attention to the extent that one can be at attention when strolling. Or was he marching at this point?

His gun now rested in his arms pointed at a forty-five-degree angle upward. He ceased when he ceased. Evidently, he'd been requested to keep nearest tabs on Francis and his exercises. Why? He had no clue.

With no intention of deliberately losing him, Francis walked directly to the cafeteria and to the buffet where he selected his poisons taken from those offered. He tailed him predictably. Like he'd been there for his entire life. Eyes directed legitimately forward and his form resolute in devotion.

When he stacked his nourishment and drink on a tray, he meandered over to an unfilled table and sat. He'd have joined his partners had any of them been in the room. Except they weren't.

CHAPTER 20.

Remaining in the stronghold was pure suicide.

When he finished eating, he found no maps or binoculars of any sort. Or, on the other hand, whatever else that may be of assistance.

He'd need to make it in isolation.

So, he wore his weapons store—total with ten hand shots—climbed himself up the stepping stool, opened the entry, and meandered out into the as of not long ago see anything tornado.

As he remained there, free as a bound flying creature, Francis glanced throughout for some sign of which heading he should look for. The most ideal way off this mountain.

As he did, it hopped out at him as a possibly that could work his way, encompassing to the contrary side of the structure to the crucial track, and then sneak himself onto the philosophy there, and tail it.

Keeping himself in an unforgiving scene unmistakably so as not to be perceived, the mountain top slant or whatever was not accommodatingly indirect and he anticipated to take a couple of detours using neighboring outcroppings and other standard bars to gain entrance.

This affected, he may not in any way shape or form come across the vanguard track, particularly given he'd reviewed the rackets of rocks falling outside, after they'd arrived proposing the entries had been disguised. So, he didn't evenhandedly glare at the mountain's zenith, or slant, or whatever, in any case outward the other course trying to discover the methodology drove him back toward progression.

He contemplated the switch-backing courses they'd taken and acknowledged which could be ordinarily trusted were broken trees and extremities revealing the method for an inquisitively huge research facility. He recalled that it hadn't come with them the whole way. They'd strolled the past leg.

Out of the blue, a voice punctuated the stillness encompassing them.

"We're bearing an assault." the walkie-talkie declared. Was it him they were inferring. Some outside infrared contraption had seen a cloud-warm body. He heard impacts not so far away, but significantly further than one might suspect.

Someone required access.

Why?

The Canadian Mounties?

The Riddle organization?

At any rate, further solicitation.

Definitely his approach of finding the course may have ousted him here, but that was against the image. Unless the ambushing force was so wanting on breaking into the mountain stronghold, they'd not observed him creeping around subsequent to them.

Potentially he could oblige them as the state armed forces within, was evidently not their job. Unluckily, were a war to truthfully start, all the examination occurred over such enormous quantities of months feasibly could be in peril. Blackie could be blown to pieces.

Francis's best course was probably pushing to sit it out in the timberland. Let the hail spread him, and detect who'd win, and what aggregate was left of their half year of isolation.

He'd about picked it was the correct approach, when the walkie-talkie bounced to life. This time the voice was absolutely prominent. Bill. Were they constrained to release the original live beasties they'd made before the timetable ran out?

"All powers should slight the indications of electromagnetism encompassing them, and hold their conditions. Above all, don't neglect what you're paid to do."

As soon as the impediment enters the internal passage, away they go. Damn him. This was a most desperate result possible. They hadn't endeavored the beasties yet and who saw what they might do? Could be ruinous and significantly and increasingly tragic than leaving the unsafe climatic deviation in its present condition.

He, by and by, acknowledged he had no risk to get out. Had to after a fashion get back within to ensure he wouldn't do it.

Should he proceed apropos the segment where the assault had obviously occurred, or return the way wherein he'd radiated and enter by techniques for the discretionary passage? The last was the most adroit strategy, as its no vulnerability would place him further from the activity and closer to Blackie to stop the discharge on the off chance that it could.

So, Francis turned and pursued his trail there. The rate of falling slush had coordinated sensibly, and the prints he'd made on his course were as of recently undeniable. Thank God, or he'd no doubt get lost.

As he charged along, the walkie-talkie, set to pass on liberal traffic about what was happening internally, required testing. So, he tested it as he walked, investigating whether the battery was still operational.

It was. It bounced out at him, one way to deal with his problem; get back in the lab was for Bill to convey a fake alert. If Francis theorized correctly, he had one of his walkie-talkies and understood it would bring him home. Was that what this was about?

Directly he did not perceive what to do.

For a second he figured out how odd he would need to be to convey original lives into the world when all reproduction gave back was questions and innovative wars. Controls for having been cogitate.

Life's a bitch and it's irrationally short.

Wasn't that an old Woody Allen joke?

If he headed down the mountain, he apparently would be caught as an uprooted individual study. He'd not crossed into Canada at a real station, however. He had no money and no distinctive evidence that was solicited in weapons. As requirements, he'd not likely make it.

Should he remain here? Take an uncovered entryway that a war had broken out and get to the lab so as to avoid the damn beasties from living impulsively, loosed on the world, and potentially imagine the 6th mass extinction event?

So, he continued after his ever-shallower impressions in the snow and peered about at the scene of generally white-verified rising above pines.

The snow changed a couple of limbs facing the turf, making it impossible to miss and unnatural anyway the dazzling shapes.

Once in some time, a lone icicle dove the completion of a lower branch into the significant snowdrifts.

Like rambling around conifer graves in an all-white burial terrain.

As he extended his thoughts, his mind coasted to Cassie. The Cassie to whom he was at present promised. He examined whether she was getting angry at him. In spite of whether she'd come across an additional person amidst the time he'd been absent from her life. In spite of whether their marriage was still on, or whether she was straightforwardly intending to marry this other individual, whatever his name was. Inside a minute he was as troubled as a hornet. In what limit may she do this to him? After all, they'd been skillful together.

Before he railed at the entire female gender, he took a couple of moments to get back some poise and turned his thoughts to something more than what's expected.

Had Jackson taken his classes like he'd done in times past? Was his lab as of not long ago working or conveyed a nonappearance of direction, withered, and the understudies exchanged to different colleges? Wasn't Cassie's family, and the head of police Patton in their little town in North Dakota inquisitive where he was, and what he may do?

He'd dismissed the flawlessness of the forested zones' ice and icicles and in only minutes had caused himself as tragic as hopeless can be.

He'd dismissed the flawlessness of the forested zones, snowflakes, icicles, and in only minutes had caused himself as tragic and hopeless as can be.

He made his past turn and looked back at the portal of the mountain city he'd lived in all through the past half year. It wasn't equal to when he'd left it. Not even proportionate. Essentially, somebody had left the portal standing open. Wide open. Didn't look great. After all, Francis had uncovered it fundamentally so no one could even contemplate its existence. Noteworthy, the snowflakes throughout the entryway had been fixed to the point where in two or three spots dead grass was punching through the crushed white stuff, and this smoothed hail created in width against gateway estimated to a swath feasibly twenty feet wide just as a gathering of animals had squashed themselves through the portal and with the dividers gone, and spread themselves out in their dash to make tracks in an opposite direction against within.

Potentially the walkie-talkie report had been proper. There had been an attack and the noises he'd heard were the originating of a veritable intrusion into the compound. And what he was eventually viewing were the impressions of the escaping acquired warriors.

He pushed the well-ordered entry careful to not add reverberations to the subtleties encompassing him.

He examined the squashed hail on the edges of what emitted an impression of presence, the free for all of humans in an all-out state of tumult. The impressions added to the knowledge that this had not been for these prints, just once in a while included heel marks with the forward push of toes striking ice endeavoring to get speed.

Desperate dread at work.

Again, he was in an episode concerning what to do.

Run?

Sneak inside to examine?

Endeavor the warring party's obvious euphoria at having rejected their workplace with so little effort?

It probably won't have truthfully been that way.

So, he pushed, apropos the entryway, against the leeward side with his edge followed against the stones to the opposite side, and as tactfully as he could, ceaselessly sneaked up on it.

The atmosphere had backed with only a few tireless snowflakes gliding down from above. He could identify a fix of blue sky all finished, and it was apparently warming a little as it ought to have been evident by the moderate streams against icicles everywhere.

When he associated at the uncovered back section, he researched. All he could find, regardless, was fogginess and separated slush puddles, as the breeze had blown it in and it had gone to water in the higher temperatures there.

Nothing else until someone in the lack of definition hollered, ". . . are you Professor Francis?"

The voice was so incredible, he dropped to his knees rapidly and bobbled with the lashes on his rifles to guarantee himself.

Cassie, his Cassie was running toward him, alive, and with her arms spread out in a hugging gesture, and life had become the most beautiful thing it could ever be.

Unless, of course, there was someone behind her ready to shoot her in the back . . .

What's added here, is that the point at which major trouble came to the surface. The alarms seemed to initialize shouting on main street trailing them. After the audience. Strong, irritable, irate sounding alarms. Multiple renditions. On their way south.

Everyone viewed toward that bearing and some even stood. Cassie gazed at him, officially choosing it was his shortcomings by one route or addition. Trying to escape their pre-marriage ceremony despite the fact that, apparently, they were at that point hitched.

He obviously had no inkling whether this had anything to do with him, yet essentially expected so. For as he observed, Patton stood and waved his arm in his direction as if he too knew, and he turned around and ran like hell. Far originating his lady of the hour.

Away taken his wedding.

Away originating the thousand or so onlookers who also he perhaps could add were assuming it was his fault.

As he ran down the aisle, he swore he heard one woman ask was he a cop, too. And the other replying, 'No, he's the one begins these wrecks the police need to fix.' Probably true.

As he passed the previous controlled column, some schmuck saluted him and said, 'Good luck, sucker!'

And out of the exercise center he went in nearby quest for Patton, and he assembled toward the alarms. How both of them anticipated to make up for mislaid futures by walking he didn't know, yet chasing each other appeared to be a smart thought.

Francis hadn't disapproved of the wedding itself so much, however, the consequences of the after-celebration were not something he was set up to suffer. Not after what had transpired to him over the past few months.

As he ran, Francis cogitated his feelings about the wedding and the deluge. He loved Cassie. And she was now safe, lovely, and his wife, He did want her to be his wife.

Would she annul their marriage by the hour he returned? These musings involved him further than what lay ahead. Something worth being thankful for, he accepted, yet better he be set up for aiding Patton than thinking about what may occur with Cassie. Or possibly not.

The traffic jam ahead of them appeared like New Year's Eve in the summertime.

The fast-revolving lights on the roofs of several police cars and the crude angles at which the cars were crammed together, the gathering of individuals fitted into the spaces between with a large portion of them wearing regalia or medical clinic costumes, or some likeness that gave no sign of what was certainly occurring.

Or had occurred.

Or was about to occur.

Or a mix of these potential outcomes.

Patton slowed the car as they approached. Waiting he supposed for any sign of trouble. But none showed at least as far as he could see.

At that point, he took Francis to his condo, halting in front. Acknowledging he had no luggage to carry and could walk well enough, even with the added weight of the cast which was plenty heavy, he offered his thanks and goodbyes, and walked the short sidewalk to his façade entryway, all the while staring at the wonderfully green lawn regularly watered by North Dakota's summer storms. No sprinklers necessary, except during droughts.

As he touched the handle of the lone doorway to his apartment, it befell to him that conceivably the bad guys had pulled a fast one on Patton. They'd arrived early and were now stationed on the other side of his door ready to shoot him as he entered. He, all the while blissfully unaware of their presence.

He stepped to one side out of range given anyone within, and stuck his key in the door lock and pushed it gently with the toe of his right shoe.

No gunfire.

No bodies flung at him.

Complete silence.

He soon-after stuck his arm out so anyone inside could see it and maybe blooper it for him, hoping as he did the cast itself could withstand the barrage of bullets fired. Still nothing. Not a peep. Not a sign anybody whose contemplation toward him was covering up in there to render their retribution for whatever he'd done to them.

Bored with his charade as a detective using his detecting skills to their fullest, he took a tentative step out in complete view of whatever lay in store for him. All this added nothing. No welcome-home party. No Cassie hanging tight to give him an embrace and a kiss. Only one major everything. What a disappointment. No trouble makers. But no good guys either.

He shut the entryway behind him, ambled to the pantry, got the quart of booze he'd put away there for familiar events, and disregarded a shot glass.

He plunked down and took a long problematic drink from the full container, swearing as he did that before it was accomplished he would be finished, too.

Of course, he'd overlooked the bedroom. Not a big bedroom as bedrooms go, though still sizeable enough for the feasible ten humans that suddenly exited its entryway into his living room screaming 'For he's a jolly good fellow' at the height of their lung's capacities.

Shit.

Other Books by David Cope

Available from Amazon, Barnes and Noble, and all good book sellers. This list does not include several hundred-published original musical scores also available from the above online sellers.

Nonfiction Books:

A Musicianship Primer
Foundations of Tonal Music
Hidden Structure: Music Analysis Using Computers
New Directions in Music seven editions.
New Music Composition out of print.
New Music Notation out of print.
Computers and Musical Style
Experiments in Musical Intelligence second edition.
The Algorithmic Composer
Virtual Music
Computer Models of Musical Creativity
Techniques of the Contemporary Composer
Computer Generated Novels

Novels

Novels in the Doug Cassidy Series archeological mysteries.:

    1: *The Death of Karlin Mulrey*
    2: *In Time for Death*
    3: *Death at Last*

Novels in the Will Francis Series computer life mysteries:

    1: *Not By Death Alone*
    2: *Death By Proxy*
    3: *Mind Over Death*

4: *Death Be Thy Name*
5: *And Death Comes Searching*

Standalone Novels:

Where Thunder Sleeps
A Winter's Keep
The Ballad of Willy Brice
Dark Money
To Keep and Bear Arms
The Last American
Cave of the Winding Stair
Thriller
The Deep Web
The Renegade Assassin
Unnamed Sources
Three Aces, One Rook, And A Kleptomaniac
Take Back Our Country
The One
Sometime, Somewhere
Beyond the Beyond
Slaughterhouse Island
Jessica
Testament
To Where Your Lifeless Bodies Go
Lucy

Computer Generated Novels.

Deep Six
No Warning
Cathy Tallpine
Honor Bound
Back Story
Crushed Ice
Snow Walker
Darkest Hour

Collections novels.

Invictus - Cassidy.
The Genesis Machine - Francis.

Books of Poems:

Comes the Fiery Night 2,000 Haiku
Of Gossamer Ghosts 200 poems
Forsooth the Dragon Has No Teeth 200 poems with drawings
Sonnets 64
Fear Not Evil 2000 Haiku

Books of Short Stories:

Of Blood and Tears 23 short stories
The Long Road Home 17 short stories
Light and Shadow 18 short stories
My Gun is Loaded 18 short stories
Night Must Fall 25 short stories
The Big Frame 21 short stories
The End of Words 21 short stories
The Impossible Man 18 short stories
Rachel's Child 30 short stories
Madam President 34 short stories
Mystery 9 short stories

Plays in Book Form

8-10-minute Plays
Seven Plays

Books of Art

Ars Ingenero
Ars Ingenero Duo
Ars Ingenero Tribus

Ars Ingenero Quattuor
Ars Ingenero Qunque
Ars Ingenero Sex
Ars Ingenero Septem
Ars Ingenero Octo
Ars Ingenero Novem
Ars Ingenero Decem
Ars Ingenero Undecem
Ars Ingenero Duodecem
Ars Ingenero Tredecem
Ars Ingenero Quattuordecem
Ars Ingenero Quindecem
Ars Ingenero Sedecem
Ars Ingenero Septendecem
Ars Ingenero Duodeviginti
Ars Ingenero Undeviginti
Ars Ingenero Viginti
In Search of a Bronze Sculpture

Children's Books

A Life
School Day
Sun, Moon, Stars
Tom's Thumb
A Penny's Worth
Bully Boy
Away Again Home
Magic
Daisy, Daisy
Gambit

Autobiographies

Tinman
Tinman Too
Tinman Tre

Books of Photographs

Requiem for Bosque Redondo
The Trees of Chimayó
The Towers of Santa Fe
Shadows of Santa Cruz
The Chimes of Carmel
The Stones of Sonoma
Big Sur Artists
The Trash of Santa Clara
The Ghosts of Monterey
The Sirens of Farallon Islands
The Bells of Saint Mary's
Light On Water

Books of Original Board Games

Taking Sides
VeriChess
How to Play Tesseract

Books on Radio Astronomy

Pleiades

100 or so books so far, not counting multiple editions.

Several of above books translated into Japanese, Spanish, and
    German;
Over 40 CDs of music;
Over thirty articles in major journals;
Nine Chapters in Books;
Many scores of music.